RANCOROUS

RANCOROUS

FRANCIS JOHN BALDUCCI

THE LIBRARY OF CONGRESS
Control Number: 1-1940819091

Balducci, Francis John, 1964–
rancorous / Francis John Balducci

ISBN 0692343407
ISBN-13 978-0-692-34340-1

Front and rear cover designs, images and elements by the author.

Printed in the United States of America.

Dedication

To my mother—every ugly word of it.

We need criminals to identify ourselves with, to secretly envy and to stoutly punish. They do for us the forbidden, illegal things we wish to do.

Karl A. Menninger

Chapter 1

"Lee, we know you're in there," the Tipton County sheriff said through a bullhorn. "Your house is surrounded. We also know your little boys are in there with you. So, surrender peacefully now."

Lee Beltrane is a man wanted in Indiana and Tennessee for bank robbery, felony assault, and forgery. His visit home was intended as a brief one—to take an extra pistol and a shot gun, clothes, and some food. In this stop, he also planned on saying goodbye to his three young sons and giving them instructions on where to hide out.

"Damn, son of a bitch!" Lee said when he heard the sheriff outside of his window. He carefully and slowly peers out and sees a few police cruisers and a handful of rifle-toting uniformed officers. He calls out to the back rooms where his sons are. "Boys? Gather 'round me. C'mon!"

The boys—Hank, fifteen years old, Stanley, thirteen, and Jan, twelve—emerge and get close to Lee while he's down on one knee.

"I was going to tell you to leave and run to Uncle Tim's house. I was going to come back for you after things died down. But, I think I'm a little late for all that."

"Are you going to run out shooting?" Hank asked.

"No, son. I can't see what good that will do. And, I don't want you boys to get hurt none. So, I think it's best for me to surrender."

"Yeah, I suppose that makes sense," Stanley said while nodding.

"Daddy, I'm scared," Jan said.

Lee holds him. "There's nothing to be afraid of, son. We'll see each other real soon. You'll visit me often, ya' hear? Meanwhile, stay with your Uncle Tim. He's taken good care of you before."

"All right," Jan said. He looks down at the needle tracks on his father's arm. He touches them.

"This is bullshit, papa!" Hank said.

"You hush your mouth and stop the swearing," Lee said sternly to Hank. "You need to set a good example to your little brothers." He looks at all three of them. "I want you boys to take care of yourselves, and I want you to watch each other's backs at all times. You can only depend on one other from this moment on. Do you hear me?"

"Yes," they said somewhat in unison.

"I'm going to open the door, and I want you boys to stay down, okay?"

They nod.

Lee walks over to the window.

"Sheriff, I'm coming out! Don't shoot!"

Lee opens the door slowly and carefully steps out with his hands raised. Behind him, Hank grabs a pistol and runs around Lee and out the door in front of him.

"Son! *No!*"

A deputy opens fire missing the boy, who had already dropped to the ground as the pistol bounced away from him. The deputy's bullets spray around the doorway. One bullet shatters Lee's head with extreme force. Brain matter and skull fragments project backward covering the faces of Jan and Stanley. Jan screams as Stanley displays a blank look as though he is processing the information.

"Hold your fire! Hold your fire, I said!" the sheriff ordered.

Hank runs back inside to see the horrific sight. He responds to Jan.

"Quit crying!" he shouted at him. He then picks up the shotgun.

"Don't, Hank!" Stanley said. "They will cut us to pieces." He then turns to Jan. "Keep crying. In fact, we should all cry."

Stanley rustles up some whimpering. The deputies then rush in.

"Don't move!" one of them barked.

The boys raise their hands; Jan keeps crying as Stanley continues to whimper. Hank just stares with deep anger at the deputy that killed their father. He recognizes him from outside. Stanley sees Hank's reaction to the deputy's presence, and both boys read the name on his uniform name plate: LOWE. Stanley studies this man very carefully. Hank offers a look to the deputy that conveys to him an absolute yearning for revenge.

The deputy attempts to avoid the boy's stare, but he can't seem to ignore it.

The sheriff enters.

"Awright, let's get these kids outta here, forthwith."

The officers hurry the boys outside to a marked van. Once the boys are inside, the vehicle bolts off to the sheriff's station.

At the sheriff's station, the boys are held in a special room. They have been cleaned up a little, but there are still some blood splatters on their clothes. The sheriff enters the room with pop and candy bars.

"Hello, boys. My name is Sheriff Jack McLean. I brought you some treats." He hands them out. He then scratches his head and looks them over while taking a deep breath. "Boys, I'm sorry to tell you this, but, your father's dead."

"Really, Jack?" Stanley said. "Are you sure? Maybe you should check him again."

"Now, look, your father was a pretty ruthless man, and he put himself and you boys in a very dangerous situation. Nothing else could be done. You fellas will be transported to a temporary detention facility where you will stay until the judge convenes a hearing to determine where you should be placed."

"We want to stay with our Uncle Tim," Hank said.

"We are contacting your mother in Hancock County right now. So, why don't you boys just relax awhile. You'll be off on your way real soon."

"What do you mean by 'temporary detention facility'?"

"You'll be going to a safe place, I assure you."

McLean gets up and walks toward the door.

"Fuck you!" Hank said.

McLean stops, but he doesn't turn around. He just grins and leaves the room. The door gently closes behind him.

* * *

A white van pulls up in front of the sheriff's station. The county logo is affixed on each of the doors with the words: TIPTON YOUTH DETENTION CENTER. Two uniformed men emerge from the vehicle and enter the building. A few minutes later, they return with the three boys. The men carefully escort the boys to the backseat and buckle them in.

The van drives a few miles to a stainless-steel-façade building. They usher the boys inside. In the main intake room, they are given a change of clothes, all gray in color, to carry into the shower area.

Clean and in facility clothes, while standing in the cafeteria, the boys take food trays and get in line with other youths. Since they arrived, they haven't spoken very much. Stanley urges the need for them to use hand signals, but Hank thinks the signs are a little difficult to remember. So, they largely remain quiet.

The food behind the glass partition is entirely unappealing. What appears to be meat is very dry and dark; the mashed potatoes—or what attempts to resemble the same—are watery and pale. The vegetables are so boiled that they appear limp and discolored.

"Fuck this!" Hank said aloud.

"Hank, be quite!" Stanley said. "They'll separate us."

"I don't fucking care! I'm not eating this shit!" Hank said while raising the tray.

A facility technician—a man of noticeably ample size and strength—approaches Hank in order to remove him.

"Don't fucking touch me, man!" Hank shouted at the man.

"Look, you need to come along with me, or—."

Just then, Hank strikes the man in the face with the tray with such force that the man falls backwards and onto the floor. Hank drops the tray, jumps on the man, and then repeatedly punches the downed man in the face. Blood quickly appears on the man's face and Hank's fists. Two other technicians enter the room and lift Hank off the floor. The boy swings wildly striking one in the stomach. The other man strikes Hank in the jaw sending him to the floor. Jan jumps in and shoves this man, but the man is too large for the boy's strength. Stanley grabs Jan and pulls him out of the way. Before Hank is able to get to his feet, he is placed in wrist restraints and removed from the cafeteria. Blood trickles down from his mouth as he is dragged away.

Stanley takes Jan to a seat and hushes him. He then whispers.

"Hank is out of the picture for the time being. It's just the two of us. You follow my lead and do exactly what I do. Got it?"

Jan nods.

A technician approaches them.

"Let's go. I'm taking you to your rooms now."

Jan looks at Stanley. Stanley nods at him.

Both boys walk slowly in front of the man.

While in their room, they quietly sit on bunk beds. Jan, sitting on the upper bunk, worries about Hank and where he may be. Stanley on the lower bunk is wondering when Uncle Tim will come to take them out of there. Also, he considers the layout of the facility, from what he has already seen, so that he may find security weaknesses that he may exploit and use to expedite an escape.

"I hope Hank is all right," Jan said.

"He's in isolated custody; I'm sure he's fine, the stupid dick."

* * *

A week later, at the Tipton County family courthouse, Judge Jerome P. Waller presides over the custody disposition of the three Beltrane boys. As luck has it, this case is in the hands of one of the bench's least competent—a man who recently won re-election with the highest campaign coffer and the slimmest of margins.

A heavyset, middle-aged woman stands at a table facing the bench accompanied by a man of similar age who is seated behind her.

"Estelle Beltrane?" the judge asked.

"Holloway, your honor. I took back my maiden name."

"I see. And, you're from Hancock County, Indiana, and records indicate that you are the biological mother of Henry, Stanley, and Jan."

"Yes, your honor."

"Okay. Well, Ms. Holloway, are you able and willing to provide a structured and loving home to these boys?"

"Yes, your honor. I most certain am, ah, will. I can't wait to take my dear, sweet boys home with me where they belong. Yes."

"All right, well then, I shall grant you immediate custody," the judge ordered.

The bailiff opens a side door, and the boys enter the courtroom.

"My sons!" Estelle said with her arms outstretched. "Come to momma!"

The boys look at each other and slowly walk to the woman.

"Where's Uncle Tim?" Hank asked.

"Well, he's not here."

"Well, why not?"

"Well, because I'm here to take you home with me."

"Let's get home," the man behind Estelle said as he stands. "I feel like pizza."

CHAPTER 2

"Travis, turn that fucking music down!" Estelle yelled from the backseat as the man drives her and the boys home from the courthouse.

"This is *my* car, and I'll play the goddamn radio as loud as I want to!" he retorted.

After a while on the road, Travis pulls into a parking lot.

"Why are you stopping?" she shouted.

"I told you, I want pizza!" he shouted back.

Inside, the décor is typical and grimy. They sit at a corner table with their elbows resting on a red-and-white-checker tablecloth. Travis fidgets with his fingers and kicks at his chair leg with a steady rhythm.

"Hey!" he called to the waitress. "How 'bout some service?"

She walks over while holding a check pad in one hand and clicking a pen in the other.

"What would you like?" she said in a slightly annoyed tone.

"Large pizza," he barked; "with lots of anchovies."

"I don't like anchovies," Stanley said.

"Me, too," Hank said.

"Well, then, flick 'em off," Travis responded.

The waitress walks off.

"So, what do we call you?" Stanley asked. "Dad?"

"How 'bout you call me Uncle Travis. And, I don't appreciate your fucking sarcasm." He then turns toward the waitress. "Beer."

"Got it," she responded without looking at him.

"For the table," he added. "Right away, honey." He then turns to Jan. "Hey, you're quiet. Don't you speak?"

"He shuts the fuck up and does what he's told," Hank said.

"Oh, he does, does he?" Travis said. "Well, Hank, maybe you should follow suit."

"Amen," Estelle said. "I want all you boys to shut the fuck up and to do what you're told. Your father spoiled you—that's what he did."

"Spoiled," Travis reiterated. "I'll fix that."

The waitress returns with two beers.

"No, *five* beers!" Travis points. "One, two, three, four, *five*."

"Sir, I can't serve beer to minors," she responded.

"I won't tell no one," he said.

"*Two* beers, sir."

A small bell rings from the kitchen. The waitress walks off.

"Sorry boys, I guess just your mom and me are drinking."

The waitress returns with the pizza. Hank reaches first. Estelle stabs his hand with a knife.

"Uncle Travis first," she said while Hank grasps his hand.

Travis laughs while he takes a slice. Then, Estelle takes a slice. The boys slowly take slices. Stanley begins to remove the anchovies.

"What are you doing?" Estelle asked.

"I'm taking them off," he answered.

"Oh, no you're not. I will not have you waste good food. Leave them on."

Stanley stops removing them.

"Now, let me see you take a big bite," she said.

Stanley holds the slice to his mouth.

"Go on," she ordered.

He takes a big bite and chews, never looking away from her. He then swallows doing his best to hold back a grimaced look.

"I'm not hungry," Hank said. "I ate a lot at the jailhouse."

"It was a detention center," Estelle said. "But you'll be going to jail soon enough."

"Not hungry? That's fine; more for me," Travis said.

Jan attempts to take a bite around the little fish bodies. He gags and heaves.

"You're a little woman," Estelle said. "Be a man and take a manly bite."

Jan takes a bite of the fish and immediately throws it up on the plate.

"Put that back in your mouth," Estelle said.

"What?" Jan asked.

"I said, put that back in your mouth!"

Jan takes his throw up in his fingers, places it in his mouth, and immediately swallows. He hold his mouth tightly to prevent it from re-emerging.

"That's better," she said.

* * *

They arrive at the mother's home in Hancock County. It's a medium-sized, two-story, wood-frame house in the middle of nowhere. It's considerably rundown and ugly. Several wood planks are either damaged or missing. The windows are dingy and covered by rusty screens. Some windows are cracked. The screen door is entirely discolored and barely holding on by its hinges. The brick stoop is missing bricks in important places. Two rusted-out cars without wheels are partially set in the grassy mud on either side of the property. In the driveway is a red pickup truck with scratched out, illegible words on each of the doors.

Although the house is in desperate need of woodwork and a paintjob, the truly logical choice would be to just tear it all down and start over. Estelle, however, doesn't have that kind of money. So, she continues to live in this sad excuse for a home.

To add to the blighted setting, several stray dogs freely roam around the location. They are docile, so no one seems concerned about their presence. However, they do leave their feces all over the place.

Despite the home's condition, the court considered it fit enough for the boys.

They enter through a weathered front door. After Travis and Estelle get in, the boys enter and stop when they realize their horrible new surroundings. There is no phone. They see clothes strewn on dingy rugs and dust and dog hairs accumulated in the corners. They respond to the air, which is strong with the smell of urine and mold. They look at each other as Estelle re-enters the room. A small lapdog, which appears to be blind in one eye, runs into Estelle's arms. She picks him up.

"Lester, baby!" she exclaimed at the creature. "My sweet little Lester." She lets him lick her mouth.

The brothers just look at each other.

"I'm sure glad you're here," she said to the boys with a sigh. "This place needs a cleaning in a desperate way." She closes the door behind them. "I have to keep you busy. After all, idle hands are the devil's workshop."

"Bullshit," Hank whispers to Stanley.

Estelle draws back a fist and punches Hank in the jaw sending him to the floor.

"I hear every thought; don't *fuck* with me," she said in a deep voice.

Jan attempts to help Hank up, but Hank pushes him away.

"Now, get upstairs and start by cleaning the bathroom. Then, clean the rooms up there. You had better do a spotless job or I'll cut youse in two. Everything you need is upstairs. So, get to it!"

Estelle leaves the room. The boys look at each other.

"I want to burn this place to the ground with her in it," Hank said as he wipes blood from his mouth.

"You should be quiet," Stanley said.

"Maybe we can notify the court," Jan said.

"That won't do any good," Stanley said. "They're outside this jurisdiction."

"What does that mean, dick?" Hank asked.

"It means they don't have the power to intervene, asshole. So, we're just going to have to make the best of it. Let's go, Jan."

The boys walk up the creaking steps. At the top, they encounter conditions that are worse than what they saw on the first floor.

* * *

"And take the rest of that shit in the yard and throw it in the pickup," Estelle told Hank and Jan.

Stanley, meanwhile, is inside cleaning all the scum and crud off the walls of the first floor bathroom. Estelle peers inside while she holds Lester.

"Stanley, I want you to sweep the dog hairs in the hallways."

He looks up at her.

"We're having a special treat tonight: my homemade sloppy joes," she said in a singsong. "Oh, and one thing: never, ever let Lester outside. I don't want the stray dogs to get at him."

"I'd like to see that," Stanley uttered under his breath.

"What was that?" she asked.

"What."

"What was that?"

"Nothing."

Estelle picks up the plunger and firmly strikes Stanley in the back with it. She leans down to say something; her breath reeks of grain alcohol. "If you fuck with me, I'll feed you to the dogs. There won't be a scrap of you left."

Outside, Hank gathers some loose wood from around the property. He hauls them to the yard. He finds a box of matches on a bench and he strikes one. He tosses the lit stick on the woodpile and watches as the flames rise and grow. He is mesmerized at what he sees.

Travis stumbles into the yard. He holds a nearly-empty bottle of bourbon. He sees Hank burning wood, he drops the bottle and walks over to him. He quietly picks up a fiery plank and then proceeds to beat him with it. Burning particles burst around Hank's head as he tries to shield himself from the blows. With a single strike to his head, Hank falls to the ground semiconscious. Travis drops the smoking wood and retrieves rope from the garage. He then drags the boy inside the house and to his room and leaves him lying on the floor; some smoke rises from his hair.

"What happened?" Estelle asked.

"The fucker is a firebug." Travis answered. "He's going to burn down the place."

"Oh, no, we're not going to have that!"

Travis then puts Hank on the bed and ties him to the bedposts. "There."

Estelle then turns to Stanley and Jan. "I think I need to send all you boys a message. Strip!"

Stanley and Jan look at each other.

"You heard me. Strip! All of it!"

The boys then proceed to take their clothes off. Travis giggles while he watches them. Estelle looks at Travis.

"Go lock the doors. I never want these boys outside ever again," she said.

Travis quickly locks the front and back doors. By the time he returns, the boys are standing naked in the middle of the room.

"Watch them," she ordered Travis.

"With pleasure."

She goes into the next room and returns holding a wooden paddle.

"Oh, boy!" Travis said.

"You first," Estelle said as she points to Stanley.

Stanley and Jan look at one another.

"Now!" she shouted.

"Where do you want me?" Stanley asked calmly.

"Lean up against the table and bend over."

Stanley complies. He looks at her.

"Turn away!" she ordered.

Stanley turns away and notices a travel magazine on a table. On the cover, he sees the words: "Boca del Rio: A Mexican Paradise." He looks over the sand and surf in the photograph.

Jan hides his eyes.

"No!" she told him. "I want you to watch."

Estelle winds back and slams the paddle with considerable force upon Stanley's buttocks. The boy jerks back but doesn't utter a sound. She strikes him again but only receives the same response. By the third strike, tears begin to run down the boy's face. Jan has a very difficult time watching and, by the fifth strike, Estelle orders Jan to keep watching. She stops at seven.

Jan is then in position. Even before she starts, he begins to cry.

"Oh, stop being such a little girl!" she scolded him.

After she finished, he fell to the floor. Blood trickles from his anus.

"Gee, I wish you boys didn't upset me and get me all sweaty when I need to go to work," she said as she fixes her blouse. "It's not good for my clients if I'm all disheveled."

She puts the paddle away and returns. She gives Travis a passionate kiss.

"I'll see you in the morning, babe," she said.

"Make money, baby!" he returned.

* * *

Later that night, while Travis is asleep, Stanley manages to open the door to his room. The lock is so old and flimsy that all he needed to do was to pull the knob away from the doorframe and firmly pull the door open.

As he opens the backdoor, which was unintentionally left open by Travis, he hears Lester barking upstairs. He steps out into the garage in hopes of finding a tool that he may use as a weapon.

He suddenly turns and sees Travis standing there, grinning.

"Now, what do you think you're doing?"

"I—I,"

Before Stanley can offer a word, Travis turns him around and places handcuffs on him. He then pulls the boy's pants down and bends him over.

"I'll teach you a lesson, little boy." He touches his buttocks. "Is this where your momma hurt you? Tisk, tisk. It's such a smooth ass, too."

Travis quickly removes his penis and violently sodomizes Stanley. When he is done, he grabs some rope from a shelf and then pulls the boy back to the house while the boy's pants dangle at his ankles. Travis' ejaculate runs down the boy's legs.

They enter Stanley's room. He throws the boy on the mattress. He then takes the rope and ties him to the bedposts.

"Rest well, Sleeping Beauty," he said as he leaves.

* * *

The following day, Estelle dresses Jan in girl clothes and has him walk around the house with a feather duster dusting the furniture.

"If you're going to act like a little girl, I'm going to treat you like one," she said.

Travis giggles at this.

"This is so funny, honey," he said. "This even makes me a little horny, I have to tell you."

She looks at him.

"Shall we go upstairs?" he asked.

"Hmm, sure."

"But, let's take him with us."

"Yeah, sure. C'mon Jan. Put down the duster and let's go upstairs."

Upstairs, the three enter the master bedroom. They position Jan at the foot of the bed.

"Stand here," she instructed.

The couple then take off their clothes and slowly embrace. They lie on the bed and copulate. Their act becomes increasingly aggressive. Jan attempts to turn away.

"Keep watching, boy!" she said.

"Please mom, Travis?"

"Hey, that's 'Uncle Travis' to you."

She screams so loud as she orgasms that it both startles and disgusts Jan.

* * *

"You must know, Hank, that I truly am a nice guy," Travis said as he untied him from the bed. A pistol is plainly visible wedged in his waistband. "Come help me untie Stanley."

They walk in the next room and untie him. Then, they retrieve Jan.

"Let's go outside; I want to show you boys something cool."

In the yard, Travis produces a pellet rifle.

"Isn't it pretty? And, it's quite accurate."

"Why are you showing this to us?" Stanley asked.

"I just wanted to try to bond with you boys because I think we've all had a rocky start. And, Jan, I hate that your mom dresses you up like a girl. If you act cool, I'll talk to her about it and get her to stop this. It's just not right."

Hank looks at Stanley. Jan just looks down.

"Those dogs make a mess, right?" Travis asked. "So, how 'bout we shoot a few of 'em? This 'ill be fun."

He takes out some pellets and loads the rifle.

"Okay, who's first?"

After a few moments, Hank speaks.

"I'll go first."

He takes the rifle while never taking his eyes off Travis. He takes aim and fires. A dog yelps and runs away. He takes aim at another dog. That dog yelps and runs away.

"Hey, you're good. Who's next?"

"I'll go," Stanley said. He takes aim, fires, and strikes a dog. He does it again.

"You boys are real good."

"Our Uncle Tim showed us," Hank said.

"Yeah, but I'm your favorite uncle. I want you to call me your Uncle Travis. Your first lesson is this: If you can't fuck it, kill it. I want you fellas to remember that. It's wisdom you can take right to the bank."

The boys look at each other. They appear unimpressed.

"Say, guys, I got something for you."

Travis removes three colorful pills from his shirt pocket. Each of them bear a smiley face. He holds one up.

"Do you boys know what this is?"

The boys don't answer.

"It's something real good. It's called ecstasy. It removes all anxiety and gets you real high. It's good stuff. Here."

Hank quickly takes one without much thought. Stanley is a little hesitant but takes one. Jan, showing that he is under pressure, takes one.

"I wish I had beer to give you to wash it down. But, we're all out."

They continue to shoot dogs, when they appear. They also shoot at empty beer cans. As they continue this activity, within a half-hour, they begin to experience the effects of the drug.

Hank shows signs of euphoria, smiling and dancing about. Stanley sits smiling with his legs crossed and his eyes closed. Jan looks nauseous with beads of sweat forming on his forehead. His jaws clench. Travis laughs at the boy's reactions to the drug.

Estelle enters the yard and witnesses the goings on. She clearly knows what happened, but she asks anyway.

"Travis, what the fuck did you give them?"

"Nothing."

"What did you give them?"

"Oh, stop your fussin'. It's just a little ecstasy. That's all. I'm just tryin' to show the boys a good time."

She goes inside and emerges with a broom. She begins to beat the boys with it.

"This yard is a fucking mess!" she yelled as she beat them.

Travis just sits and laughs at the boys' reactions to Estelle's violent outburst. She beats them so hard that she quickly becomes tired.

"Now, take my boys inside right now and tie them to their beds," she commanded Travis.

"Oh, c'mon, hun?"
"Do it now, I said!"

CHAPTER 3

While captive for several months, the Beltrane boys turned sixteen, fourteen, and thirteen years old, but there were no birthday indulgences for them—unless Travis regards cold, brown rice and bourbon as a celebratory meal.

Estelle made it very clear to Travis that Hank and Stanley are never to be untied at the same time. Rather, each should be untied individually to do work around the house. Hank does construction work and heavy lifting while Stanley fixes pipes and electrical fixtures. As for Jan, he just wanders about in a dress and is supervised while he does his chores, which consist mainly of sweeping, dusting, and laundry.

On one morning, the boys smell something baking in the kitchen—something good. While Travis sits in the living room watching television, Estelle unties Stanley and takes him and Jan into Hank's room. She then goes into the kitchen and returns with a tray of cornbread. It is the freshest food that they would ever receive since living there. The small, golden-brown bricks are stacked high and they smell toasty. However, the boys are hesitant to eat.

"Go on, eat," she said with a gentle a voice.

Stanley takes two and crams them into his mouth. Jan takes one and feeds it to Hank while he's still tied to his bed.

"I know that I've acted like a real bitch since you're arrived here, but I want you to know that I want things to change between us. I want you boys to be happy here."

The boys chew as they listen with blank looks— as though they are prisoners of war under negotiations with the enemy.

"Everything that I do is for your own good. We need to build trust between us. You know?"

The boys maintain their blank looks.

After she realizes that it would be pointless to continue her talk, she nods. "Well, I'll just let you boys finish up. When you're done, Stanley I need you to fix a leak in the basement and, Jan, there's some sweeping that needs to be done in the front rooms." She leaves them.

They look at each other. Hank now appreciates Stanley's advice to communicate without speaking. Although hand signals are out of the question for the time being, they resort to eye movements. With little means available to them to fully communicate their thoughts, one thing is certainly conveyed between them: she is completely full of shit.

* * *

"Yeah, right... Oh, my... Really?" Travis said over the phone. "Yeah, I can be there tomorrow, late afternoon. She, died, yeah it's too bad. But, life goes on, you know? Okay, I'll see you."

Travis runs to Estelle in the front of the house.

"Babe, my mother died, and I need to go to her house tomorrow."

"Darlin' I'm sorry."

"No, don't worry about it. It was her time. It's also *our* time to live better."

"What do you mean?"

"I inherited some cash, baby, and it's just waiting for me to pick it up."

While Jan washes the evening dishes, he leaves the kitchen with the water still running in the sink. He remembered that a dish was sitting on a table in the living room, so he goes to retrieve it.

"About two-hundred thousand dollars in cash, and I pick it up tomorrow in Terre Haute. I'll be back the following day."

Jan's eyes open wide at what he hears. He takes the plate and goes back to the kitchen to wash it.

"We'll buy a really nice house—a much better house—in Florida. We'll be by the ocean, and you'll no longer need to prostitute yourself to make ends meet."

"What about my boys?"

"We'll take 'em. It will be a better life for all of us."

They passionately kiss and embrace.

"This is so great! I'll tell them," she said.

"No, not yet. We'll tell them after I get back. It will be a surprise."

They kiss again.

Travis walks back to the living room. He notices that his plate has been removed, but he thinks little of it. He then hears the kitchen sink faucet turn off.

* * *

On the following day, Estelle from the front porch watches Travis drive off. She knows that he loves her. So, she has no concern that he would never return.

Estelle then goes inside and takes Stanley and Jan into Hank's room.

"Now, boys, Travis went away on a little business trip. He'll be back real soon, all right? I spoke with him about becoming more like a family. But, you need to earn our trust."

The boys look down.

"When Travis comes home, you will be given more freedom to walk around so long as you don't leave the house. I promise."

Hank shifts in his bed.

"Okay, I have to do a few things before dinner. Jan, why don't you finish the floors. Stanley, the table in the living room is still wobbly, so fix the legs, all right?"

Stanley and Jan rise, walk out of the room, and then get right to work. Estelle looks at Hank in the bed.

"I know you may hate me, but things will change. I'm not a monster, really."

Hank refuses to look at her.

"I'm your mother, son."

She then leaves the room without saying another word. She looks back at him as she closes the door.

While Estelle is outside hanging clothes, Stanley quietly walks back into Hank's room.

"Jan says that Travis will return with two-hundred thousand dollars in cash," Stanley said.

"I'm going to kill that fucking whore, I swear."

"Just relax. We need to cause a distraction so we all can escape. Then, we'll return for the money and Travis' car."

"I have a better plan. Just go back to Jan and get ready for all hell to break loose."

"What are you going to do?"

"Just shut the fuck up and do what I say."

Stanley is so tired that he doesn't have the strength to argue. He nods at Hank, leaves his room and closes the door.

Estelle is in the kitchen dressing a chicken for the oven. She sees Stanley.

"Son, it's time for you to go to bed so Hank can do some chores. Let's go."

"Okay, mother."

She ties him to his bed and closes the door. She then enters Hank's room and unties him.

"I need you to move the furniture in the living room. We're going to paint the walls."

"Sure."

Hank's foot appears to be asleep, so he walks slowly with a slight limp. Estelle sees this and goes to the kitchen to put the chicken in the oven.

Hank sees Jan and quickly approaches him.

"I'm going to do something, let's say, very aggressive. But, I will come back for you and Stanley."

"What do you want me to do?"

"Nothing. Just stay the fuck out of the way."

"But, Hank, she said she will treat us better when Travis returns. She's our mother, and I think she deserves a chance."

"Wake the fuck up, you dick! You're dressed like a fucking girl, for Christ's sake!"

* * *

While Hank is moving furniture to the center of the floor, he often looks toward the kitchen to where his mother is. He sees her open the oven and shake spices over the bird, and then she places it back into the oven. He then sees what he needs—a carving knife.

He slowly and carefully creeps up to the kitchen doorway. His heart pounds inside of his chest; he can feel it in his throat. He looks inside.

"What are you doing here?" she asked him.

"I just wanted to know if you need any help."

"No, I don't. I can do a simple thing like roast a chicken."

"Okay, just asking."

"Are you finished in there yet?"

"Almost."

"Well, hurry up; we're going to eat soon."

Hank then goes back into the living room and moves a table a few inches. He then feels the rage build up inside of him. His heart begins to pound again. He stealthily runs into the kitchen, grabs the knife that was sitting on a carving board, and quickly stabs her in the breast. The act causes a superficial wound because the knife doesn't fully penetrate her chest. Like a wounded animal, she lets out a guttural yell as she falls to the floor.

He swiftly kicks the rear door in an attempt to force it open. He makes two attempts with no success.

As she tries to get to her feet, she reaches for a small drawer. From it, she produces a pistol. She hastily fires, but the bullet strikes the wall above his head as he breaks through the door. She hobbles over to the doorway so she can shoot him in the yard, but he had already escaped into the darkness of the night.

"You *fuck*!" she yelled out into the yard.

* * *

In the morning, after Estelle had already hid all of the kitchen knives, Stanley finishes fixing the rear door. Her dried blood is present on her housedress. She plainly carries the pistol in one of its pockets.

Estelle inspects his handy work. After she is satisfied, she then returns Stanley to his room and ties him to his bed.

Jan, meanwhile, remains locked in his room. When she enters, she notices a strong odor.

"What did you do?"

"Nothing, mom."

"Did you shit yourself?"

"I—I."

"Eat it."

"Wha—?"

"I said, eat it!"

Jan removes his dress and then his underwear. He removes the feces and takes it into one hand.

"Go on!"

Jan takes the blob into his mouth.

"Chew it!"

He sees the bulge of the pistol in her housedress pocket and begins to chew.

"You're a disgrace," she said as she left the room.

He immediately throws up. He kneels down and uses his dress to clean the floor. Then, he goes to the dresser and removes a replacement dress from the drawer and puts it on.

Chapter 4

It's a day later, and we find Stanley and Jan cleaning together in the front room. They know that Estelle is nearby—perhaps even in listening distance—and that, after Hank's stunt, she may still have a pistol in her direct possession. So, their immediate endeavor is to plan their mother's murder without uttering a single word about how to do it. They resort to using hand signals and, with their lives at stake, they find themselves quite fluent in this form of communication.

Stanley emphasizes to Jan that they must factor out Hank's involvement in their plan. For all they know, he may be wounded and lying somewhere bleeding to death in the woods. Stanley also insists that they must act fast before Travis returns. Two on two without weapons stacks the odds way too high against them. Stanley conveys the need for a distraction.

There has always been a sort of innocence that

resided within Jan. However, with serious hate and conviction in his eyes, and without the least bit of reservation, he offers a confident nod to Stanley's plan.

Nearby, they hear a slight creak from a floorboard in the next room. They quickly realize that Estelle is closer to them than they wish.

"I don't know what you are doing in there; it certainly isn't cleaning. So, Stanley, let's pick up the clothing that Travis was nice enough to throw around."

She then walks into the room and sees Jan.

"I want you in bed," she told him. "Stanley, keep working."

She takes Jan into his room, turning twice as she walked down the hallway. She tied him to his bed. She then went into the kitchen to make herself an herbal tea. While she does this, she peeks out from the kitchen doorway to spy on Stanley. She sees him picking up clothes on the floor and placing them in a frayed wicker basket. She thinks he looks sickly, probably due to malnutrition. What she is not aware of is that, although he isn't entirely well, he is indeed acting frail and weak in an attempt to cause Estelle to lower her guard. The tea kettle whistle blows, so she goes to the stove.

Lester, who is sitting half-asleep on a plush chair in the living room, closes its eyes. Stanley reaches down and quickly picks up the animal, opens the front door, and tosses it outside. Its little head hits the gravel so hard that it quickly becomes disoriented. Stanley closes the door as quietly as he opened it.

Just outside, they hear the sound of growling, scurrying dogs.

"Those fucking dogs!" Estelle responded to the commotion not knowing that her dog is outside.

* * *

Estelle hears the washing machine chime in the basement indicating that the load is done.

"Stanley, be a lamb and bring the clothes up."

As he does this, she returns the teacup to the kitchen.

While in the basement, Stanley looks around for something that he can use as a weapon. All he can muster is a piece of thin plastic pipe that Travis left behind when he was supposed to throw it away. Estelle directed Travis to remove all items that she thought may be used to help facilitate the boys' escape.

He places the item in the basket, and then he puts the clothes on top of it. When he returns to the living room, he carefully removes the pipe from the basket and drops it behind the couch.

Just then, Estelle enters the room.

"I'll take that," she said as she took the basket from him. "I'm going to hang these on the line."

As soon as she leaves the house, Stanley ran to Jan's room. He turned its doorknob to learn that the door is locked. He then runs to the living room, obtains the pipe, and stands at the front door and readies himself. He takes a deep breath.

"*Lester*!" she screamed when she finds the dog's shredded, mangled body in the driveway. She quickly goes inside to confront Stanley.

As she enters, Stanley draws the pipe back and strikes her in the head with severe force. She stumbles to the floor on one hand as she reaches into the pocket of her housedress with her other hand to obtain the pistol. She draws it, but then drops it in front of her. It bounces away from them. He attempts to obtain it by leaping for it like a toad, but she manages to kick him in the groin sending him to the floor.

She tries to rise and walk, but Stanley gets up and jumps behind her. He then removes his tee-shirt and wraps it around her neck. He squeezes tightly—as tightly as his small body is able. The tighter he squeezes, the more her eyes bulge from their sockets. As she struggles for air, her face glows red. White foam develops from around her mouth. She tussles so violently that much of her housedress tears from her body. Their exposed skin creates such a bizarre visual that it resembles two animals battling in the wild.

After she regained some forward movement, she obtains the pistol. She fires backwards without looking, but the bullet harmlessly embeds itself into the ceiling above Stanley's head.

Jan calls out from inside his room.

Stanley then grabs the pistol firmly. It fires again. The bullet grazes his cheek causing a superficial burn. He pries the weapon from her hand, points it at the back of her head and pulls the trigger. It misfires. He then uses the butt of the pistol to strike her in the head. He strikes her so hard that he feels his knuckles crackle. He then drops the pistol and resumes his strangle hold.

She stands up for a moment, but only to then fall forward onto a porcelain lamp that sits on a small table. The lamp shatters. He again mounts her, reaches down, and then takes a shard and draws it across her throat. As she bleeds out, she becomes limp and lifeless until she stops moving.

Stanley rolls off of her and collapses onto the floor. He draws in a deep breath and calls out.

"Jan, it's done! I'll free you in a few minutes!"

He then thinks of Travis.

"Jan, I'm coming over now!"

* * *

As Stanley unties Jan, his brother begins to cry.

"Jan, there is a time and place for everything, and this is neither the time nor the place. We need to prepare the house for Travis. If he sees the dead woman in the middle of the room it will eliminate the element of surprise, don't you think?"

In the living room, they look down on the corpse. She is a big, bloody mess.

"The pistol is over there. It jammed, so clear it the way Uncle Tim taught you."

Jan picks up the pistol and clears the jam. He hands the pistol to Stanley who wedges it into his waistband.

"What do we do with her?" Jan asked.

"We drag her—down the hallway into the bathroom. Then, we clean up this room and ourselves."

"Travis is going to notice a table and lamp missing."

"I know that, but maybe he won't fully notice. Besides, it was a small table. Let's go; get her legs."

The two lift with all of their strength and slowly drag the body. They exert themselves, heaving, while breathing heavy. The linoleum floor in the hallway makes the task slightly easier. They enter the bathroom and drop her head and legs with a thud. Stanley looks at Jan's bloody dress.

"I bet you can't wait to get out of that thing."

"I forgot that I was wearing it."

"Yeah, well first we need to clean up. Then we can launder these clothes, shower, and then put on clean clothes. We're also going to need more bullets for this gun, and maybe we can find another gun upstairs. If we do find another one, there is a good chance that it will be loaded. Here." Stanley grabs a mop and bucket near the toilet and hands it to Jan. "I think there's some bleach under the sink," he said. He grabs the bottle and, together, they walk down the hallway.

Jan gets the garbage can from the kitchen. They then get to work cleaning up the mess.

An hour later, they sweep up the last bits of debris. They then light a scented candle to mask the strong bleach smell. Stanley then directs Jan to go upstairs and take a shower while he stands watch.

Fifteen minutes later, Jan returns downstairs looking cleaner and dressed in his old clothes. Stanley hands him the pistol and a box of stale cold cereal.

"Now, if Travis returns while I'm upstairs, you only have one bullet in the chamber. So, hide yourself well, jump out near him, and shoot him in the chest. Then, run out the back door. I'll come down and finish him off. Got it?"

"Got it."

Stanley goes upstairs. After his shower and change of clothes, he looks around the master bedroom. There, he finds a loaded pistol and more ammunition hidden on a high shelf in a closet. Next to it, he finds an old, stained shoebox. In it, he finds about five thousand dollars in cash and the title to Travis' car. In Estelle's dresser, in some of its drawers, he finds more cash and some jewelry. He also finds the house keys. He takes all the items, puts them in a plastic bag, and then goes downstairs to join with Jan.

"All quiet," Jan told him.

"Good. Say, I'm going to check the garage. We were never allowed in there, and I'm a bit curious why. Here's more bullets, so load up."

As Jan loads his pistol, Stanley instructs him a little more.

"Now you have more bullets. So, this time, when you pop out, shoot the shit out of him."

"Okay. No problem."

Stanley opens the back door and walks to the garage. He opens the wide door. In the far corner, on a dusty work bench, he sees a white cloth spread open. He lifts it to find below all of the kitchen knives that Estelle had hidden. They lie carefully aligned and shiny. He then looks up and sees a hatchet mounted on the wall. He also finds some rope and twine. In the corner, he sees the pellet rifle and a box of pellets.

Stanley comes up with an idea. He covers the knives, picks up the pellet rifle and the box, and goes back inside the house with Jan to wait for Travis to return with his money.

* * *

On the following day, Travis pulls into the

driveway. He steps out of his car and walks up the steps wearing a broad smile and carrying a large bottle in a brown bag. He opens the door and steps into the house.

"Estelle?"

Stanley and Jan then emerge from the kitchen. Stanley smiles while Jan offers a hateful look.

"Uncle Travis," Stanley said; "we missed you so much."

"Boys, where's your mother?" Travis said with a confused expression.

"Let's just say she's in the bathroom."

Travis then goes into his waistband for something. Jan draws his pistol and points it at him.

"What did you bring, uncle? Bourbon? Here, let me have that."

Stanley takes the bag from him and opens it.

"Hey, this must be the expensive kind. Moving up into the world, are we?"

"Now, boys, what's this all about?"

"What do you mean, uncle? We're just real glad to see you—real glad. In fact, your return home to us calls for a celebration. Put your hands up."

"Hold on, fellas, I'll give you anything you want," he said as he raises his hands. "I can give you some money."

"Oh, Uncle Travis, we don't want *some* of your money. That wouldn't make any sense, now would it?" Stanley goes into Travis' waistband and pulls out his pistol. He checks it and finds it fully loaded, and then puts it in his own waistband.

"Cover him well," Stanley said softly to Jan.

Jan nods at Stanley and points his pistol directly at Travis' face. Stanley searches Travis and takes his keys and wallet. He also finds a small knife and puts it in his pocket.

"Uncle Travis, how 'bout we go downstairs into the basement and party? We have a nice little setup for us there. It'll be fun."

"Boys, *please*?" I beg you."

"Aw, c'mon. Jan and I are trying so hard to be good hosts for your triumphant homecoming, and we think it's highly disrespectful to turn down our sincere hospitality."

Stanley then conveys a hateful gaze deeply into Travis' eyes.

"I said, let's go downstairs into the basement."

Travis then walks slowing behind Stanley. Jan follows with his pistol pointed at the back of Travis's head.

In the basement, a small chair is secured to a support beam.

"Have a seat, Uncle Travis."

"But—"

Stanley draws his pistol and puts it in his face.

"Sit!" Stanley takes a deep breath. "We don't want you to call the police after we leave. We want a good distance from this place before we call someone and tell him where you are. So, just sit the fuck down, all right?"

Travis, with his hands raised, sits in the chair.

Stanley takes Jan's pistol.

"Tie him—like I taught you how."

Jan ties Travis to the chair. His arms are secured behind his back while his waist is bound to the chair and his ankles are fixed to the chair legs. Stanley gives Jan both pistols and tests Jan's work.

"Good job, Jan. He's snug."

"Now, you boys are going to go, right?"

"Well, not yet. Jan, hand me that thing over there."

"Hand you what thing?" Jan said with a smile.

Stanley laughs. "Oh, you know what thing."

"Oh, *that* thing." Jan produces the pellet rifle and hands it to Stanley.

"Now, c'mon, boys. You were supposed to just leave me here. Now what are you doing?"

Stanley turns to Jan. "It's loaded?"

"Yeah, all ready to go."

"All right, hold these and keep him covered." Stanley hands Jan both pistols. He then gets down on one knee and aims the rifle directly at Travis' face."

"Uncle Travis, did you know that I love dogs?— except for Lester. I hated that fucking dog. That's why I killed it."

Stanley squeezes the trigger. A pellet strikes Travis in the cheek.

"Aaaahhhh!" Travis screamed. Blood quickly trickles from the small wound.

"Yeah, I killed that little dog. Then I killed Estelle."

Stanley squeezes the trigger again. A pellet strikes Travis in the other cheek.

"Aaaaaahhhh!"

"Uncle Travis, have you ever met someone who murdered his own mother?"

Stanley squeezes the trigger again. A pellet strikes Travis in the chin.

"Aaahhhrr!"

"No? Well, you have now."

Stanley squeezes the trigger again. A pellet strikes Travis in the forehead.

"Aaaahhh!"

"Jan, this isn't happening quick enough." Stanley puts down the rifle and stands. He reaches into his pocket and pulls out Travis' small knife. He cuts open Travis' pants and exposes his penis.

"Gee, Uncle Travis, the last time I saw this little thing you were about to fuck me in the ass with it."

"Fuck you!" Travis said. As he spoke, his blood splatted from the wounds on his face.

"Fuck me? You already have."

"Rrrruuuggg!" Travis grunted as he struggles in the chair.

"You know, for the rest of my life I will have the image in my mind of you fucking me in the ass. I need to replace that with a new image."

Stanley reaches down, pulls on Travis' penis, and removes it from his body with one slice of the knife.

"Aaaaaaaahhhhhhgggg!"

Stanley holds the severed penis in front of Travis' face.

"I bet you never saw this thing this much up close. Have you?"

"Stanley, give me that. And give me the knife and take the pistols."

"What, Jan?"

"Please?"

"Oh, okay?"

Stanley and Jan make the exchange.

"Uncle Travis, my mother taught me that when you make a mess, you have to eat it," Jan said while holding the penis to Travis' face. Jan pries Travis' mouth open with the knife and shoves the penis way inside. He crams it deeper into his throat with the blade.

Travis immediately gags and attempts to spit it out. But, the meaty morsel is so deep inside his throat that he gags on it. After a few convulsive jerks, Travis loses consciousness and slumps over.

"Brother, I'm so proud of you," Stanley said. "That was genius. Honestly, I wasn't sure how to end this creatively, and you followed through quite nicely. Well played, sir."

Jan looks up at Stanley and smiles at him. Stanley smiles back and then checks Travis' vital signs.

"Now, let's get him upstairs and in the bathroom, Jan."

They untie the corpse and carry it upstairs to the bathroom. They lay it right next to the other one.

"Whelp, time to clean up again," Stanley said. "We'll start with the basement, and then we'll launder our clothes and shower again. Then, we need to locate Travis' money and load up all the other valuables in his car."

"What about Hank?"

"I guess we'll give him until morning. If he doesn't show up, we'll have to make haste with the bodies and get moving."

"I hope he's all right."

They close the bathroom door.

* * *

Early the next morning, Hank pulls up near the house in a stolen car after he sees Travis' car in the driveway. He then carefully walks over to the house. Jan sees him from a window.

"Hank! We're safe! Come in!"

Hank smiles, waves, and then goes back for the stolen car. He drives it deep into the yard.

When Hank enters the house, Jan gives him a hug. Hank smiles at him and then looks around.

"What happened?"

"We have a lot of money!" Jan said.

Stanley appears from the kitchen.

"Where have you been?" Stanley asked.

"I got lost in the woods. I ran until I saw civilization. I stole a car, and here I am. Where are they?"

"In the bathroom," Stanley said.

"Dead?"

"Quite dead."

"Good, that's good. I called Uncle Tim a few days ago. When we reach Tipton County, he is willing to help us."

"That's good."

"So, where are the bodies?"

They walk to the back and open the bathroom door. Hank sees them. They have already started to decompose, and the smell hits them hard.

"We need to dispose of them," Stanley said. "If court officials come by to check on us, they will know we did this and they'll be after us."

"Let's burn them," Hank said.

"That will bring way too much attention to this place. I have a better idea: we need to chop them up into small pieces and feed them to the dogs. Not much will be left of them; they'll be dog shit in about a week."

"How will we do this?" Jan asked.

"Jan, we'll take off all our clothes. Then, we'll work in the bathroom cutting the bodies up into parts and throwing them out the window into the yard. Hank, you'll be in the yard where you'll chop those parts up into smaller pieces. Throw those pieces to the dogs. It's that simple. Everything we need is in the garage; there are knives and a hatchet. Okay?"

Jan nods.

Hank nods. He then smiles.

* * *

After a half-hour, Stanley and Jan vigorously work in the bathroom. Stanley offers Jan some instruction.

"It's easier if you cut at the joints. Let Hank work on the big bones."

Like a morbid assembly line, they toss the parts out the window. They fall to the ground. Hank, dressed in his underwear, then chops the parts into small pieces and feeds them to the dogs. The animals' numbers grow with each passing minute.

"Gee, these dogs are eating well," Hank said with a smile while holding the bloody hatchet.

"Fresh meat!" Stanley quipped. "Keep on chopping!"

Stanley recalled that the stray dogs only mangled Lester. However, he now realizes that the dogs are showing no concern or hesitation about eating human flesh.

* * *

Smelling fresh, the Beltrane boys load up Travis' car with some food, clothes, Travis' bourbon, and nearly a quarter of a million dollars in cash and valuables. They also take the pistols, ammunition, and Travis' handcuffs. Hank gets behind the wheel of this car.

Stanley gets behind the wheel of the stolen car and takes Jan with him. The intention is to drive to a nearby remote location and ditch it, and then get in Travis' car and drive to Uncle Tim's house.

They depart.

One-half mile from the house, a Hancock County deputy sheriff cruiser appears. The officer pays no mind to Hank. However, he does see Stanley and quickly realizes that the driver looks way too young. The officer gestures for him to pull over. Stanley complies.

While Hank looks in his rearview mirror, he sees Stanley get pulled over. Yet, he keeps on driving.

CHapteR 5

Stanley sits in the guest's chair in the sheriff's office. He looks around the well-appointed place and notices various plaques and documents hung evenly spaced on the mahogany walls. He looks down and notices a framed picture sitting prominently on his huge desk. The image is of a handsome young man and a pretty young woman. They appear to be on vacation on a sailboat somewhere. But before Stanley can get a closer look, a uniformed man enters the room.

"Hello, son. I'm Sheriff Earle Brooks."

"Hello. I'm *not* Sheriff Earle Brooks."

Brooks laughs. "No, you're not. You're Stanley Beltrane, and I have a few questions that I'd like for you to answer, all right? First off: why were you driving a stolen car?"

"I was just trying to leave town."

"Now, why's that?"

"Well, sheriff, there's really no need for me to continue to live in Hancock County."

"Why not?"

"Because my mother left me for good. So, what would be the point?"

"Why would your mother leave? You seem like a nice boy."

"My mother hated the house that she was living in because it is rundown and falling apart. She kept talking about moving."

"Did she mention that she was going to take you and your brothers with her?"

"Every time we asked, she would just change the subject."

"I see." Brooks scratches his chin. "Go on."

"Well, one night, I overheard a conversation she had with her boyfriend, Travis—or at least that's the name he told us. Anyway, he told her that he was inheriting a huge amount of money. He also talked about moving to Boca del Rio, Mexico."

"When was this?"

"About a week ago. We haven't seen the two of them for five days. So, we decided to leave—no point in staying in a house we would eventually be evicted from for not paying taxes."

"What about your brother, Hank? What happened to him? Where is he?"

"Hank ran off when he had a bit of an argument with our mother. Before he left, he said something about Key West."

"I see, well, Deputy Rory will step in and keep you company. Are you hungry? Thirsty?"

"Grape pop, please? And a Snickers bar?"

"Okay, I think we can rustle that up for you. Just sit tight."

"Will do, Sheriff Earle Brooks."

Brooks smiles. He then leaves and closes the door behind him. Stanley takes a deep breath.

In the communications room, Brooks orders the broadcast of an all-out report on Henry Beltrane. He includes in the report that the youth may be on foot and, perhaps, could be headed somewhere south.

Brooks then enters another room where Jan sits at a table eating a fast-food burger and drinking a cola.

"Hello, Jan. I'm Sheriff Earle Brooks."

"Hello, sir," he said while chewing.

"So, where were you going when my deputy stopped you?"

"We were looking for our brother, Hank."

"Where do you think he is?"

"I don't know. He's been gone for a while. He was never happy in that house."

"You have no idea where he is?"

"No, sir."

"What about your ma?"

"Oh, she left a few days ago. She may be gone for good."

"Why's that?"

"She was always unhappy—especially with me. I guess she didn't want to be our momma no more."

"Okay, son. Finish up and, when you're done, we're going to take you to somewhere safe." Brooks gets up to leave.

"Sheriff?"

He turns. "Yeah?"

"When you find my mom, please don't blame her for leaving."

"Now don't you worry about that." He offers the boy a gentle, reassuring smile before he leaves.

* * *

A minivan pulls up in front of the sheriff's station. Two men emerge from the vehicle and enter the brick building. Minutes later, two men escort Stanley and Jan into the vehicle. These men then enter, and the minivan slowly rides away.

In the shadows a car materializes. It follows the minivan until both vehicles disappear into the night.

* * *

Two days later, inside the sheriff's station, Brooks compiles his preliminary report. He goes into his office and calls inside his chief investigator. He places the file on his desk, opens it, and when the officer enters he dictates the information to him.

"Carl, statewide authorities can't seem to locate Estelle Holloway. We know that she has a boyfriend named Travis Elkner, and that this man did indeed inherit a large sum of money from his deceased mother. His truck is still at the residence, but the car is nowhere to be found. Here's the information on it." He shows the investigator a computer printout of the car's data. "I imagine he sold this rusty can before his trip. My guess is that they're gone for good."

"How much money did he inherit?"

"His sister said about two-hundred thousand dollars. She seemed pretty pissed off when she told us."

"I guess she got shit."

"Reckon so. After seeing the shit box that Holloway and Elkner were living in, my guess is that they simply up and left."

"She abandoned her boys?"

"It sure looks that way. Stanley, the middle boy, said he overheard them talking about moving to Boca del Rio, Mexico."

"Boca del Rio? Sounds good to me, sheriff. Anything on the oldest boy? What's his name? Henry? Hank?"

"Nothing. Well, he may be headed somewhere south." He scratches his head. "Nothing yet."

Chapter 6

The youth detention facility of Hancock County is much cleaner and much less crowded than the one in Tipton County. Even the food is better.

To Stanley, one important thing about this place is that the security is rather *laissez-faire*. At night, there is usually one guard, probably underpaid, and most-likely uninspired.

On one occasion, Stanley looked out of the window to see Hank parked in Travis' car. Stanley shook his head at him. On another occasion, Stanley hand-signals him three fingers and an "okay" sign. Hank understands Stanley's message and returns with a thumb up.

Stanley approaches Jan. "I saw him again—a half-hour ago."

"He hasn't left us."

"No. It's on. We need to slip out at three a.m. He will be waiting for us. Only one guard will be on duty, and that one usually sleeps in his chair at that hour. So, I think this may be quite easy for us to pull off."

"Okay. I'll be ready."

* * *

As anticipated, the guard is asleep in his chair. To maximize their stealthy efforts, Stanley and Jan time their movements by the man's loud snores.

Stanley gently opens the rear door not expecting an alarm to sound, but he's prepared for it nonetheless. Quiet. "C'mon, hurry!" he whispered to Jan in case he triggered an inaudible signal.

Both boys scale a tall fence and find themselves on the sidewalk. Hank pulls up with the headlights off. They swiftly board, and then Hank quickly accelerates.

"Hey, douchebags!" Hank said with a smile as he turns on the headlights.

"Hey, dick breath!" Stanley retorted. "May I suggest that we get out of this county before morning?"

"Way ahead of you, brother. We're making our way to Uncle Tim."

Hank gets on a major highway making certain not to exceed the speed limit.

As day breaks, they find themselves in Madison County. While Jan sleeps in the backseat, Hank sees a rundown motel. Stanley sees it, too. The vacancy sign is illuminated.

"They probably accept cash, no questions asked," Stanley said.

Hank nods and pulls into the rear parking lot.

"I'll be back with the key," Hank said.

A few minutes later, he returns with the key and a few cans of pop.

Inside the room, Jan goes back to sleep. Stanley also gets some rest. Hank, however, stays up to watch Tom and Jerry cartoons as he drinks his third can of Coke.

* * *

After Brooks received the call that the Beltrane boys left the facility, he throws his phone against the wall.

"What the fuck kind of place are they running there. *Jesus Christ!* They can't fucking watch two boys?"

Brooks orders the broadcast of an all-out report on all three Beltrane boys.

He gets in his cruiser and drives. He just drives. He searches for the boys completely believing that he won't really find them by merely driving around.

* * *

Later that afternoon, Hank leaves Stanley and Jan to go for supplies: snack cakes, beer, and cigarettes.

Hank drives on a desolate road at about fifty-five miles per-hour. He wants to drive a little faster, but this time his attention is preoccupied by the driver in an SUV tailgating him. The sight of the vehicle dominates his rearview mirror.

Hank slows down to try to shake him off, but the motorist continues on his tail. Hank slows down more, to forty-five. Finally, the SUV swiftly passes him while driving dangerously close—almost sideswiping him.

After less than a minute, as Hank drives around a sharp turn, he sees the SUV overturned and smoking. A few feet from the wreckage, he sees the motorist on the asphalt bleeding from the head but moving— still alive. Hank pulls over. He exits his car and slowly walks over to the injured man.

"Do you know me?" Hank asked.

The man is puzzled by the question. "No," the man answered in a weak voice.

Hank returns to his car and opens the trunk. He removes a crowbar and walks back to the injured man. He approaches the man and, without uttering another word, he repeatedly strikes him in the head until much of the man's brain is exposed. Upon completion, he takes a moment to admire his work.

"Such a horrible accident," he said. "Too bad."

He retrieves the man's wallet from his back pocket, takes the cash, and puts the wallet back.

Hank tosses the crowbar back into the trunk and drives off.

Minutes later, he arrives at a convenience store. He goes into the restroom to wash off much of the blood, brain matter, and skull fragments. He exits the restroom, grabs all that he needs and approaches the counter.

"Let me also get a carton in Marlboro red."

"I need to see your ID for the beer," the clerk said.

"No, you don't." he said while he places the items on the counter.

"Yes, I do."

"Would you rather see a bullet strike you in the middle of your forehead?" He shows the pistol wedged in his waistband.

The clerk raises his hands. "Hey, I'm just doing my job."

"Well, how 'bout a new job?"

"What's that?"

"Well, your new job is to be my bitch. Let's see if you know how to be my bitch."

"I don't understand."

"Be my bitch and open the cash register."

"The cash register?"

"Yeah, open it before I fire you for insubordination."

The clerk opens the cash register.

"All of it, bitch! Let's go!"

The clerk hands him all the cash. Hank quickly tucks it into his pants.

"Two things: you don't tell the police about me or I'll come back and blow you away without saying a fucking word. You got it?"

"But, I have to tell the owner something."

"Tell him it was some big, black guy. Second thing: the next time someone underage wants to buy beer, just sell it to him and shut the fuck up. Okay?"

"Okay, no problem."

Hank removes some cash and counts out two hundred dollars. He gives it to the clerk. "Here, I think you've earned your pay."

Hank leaves smiling.

The clerk, with shaking hands, puts the money into his pocket.

* * *

57

Later that afternoon, the Beltrane boys travel to Tipton County. They arrive at Uncle Tim's house. From his window, Tim sees the boys pull up. He steps outside to greet them.

"Hank, put the car in the backyard," Tim said. Tim follows the car into the back. He ushers them inside through the backdoor and to the dining room. "When was the last time you boys had a hot meal?"

"It's been too long, uncle," Hank said.

"Have a seat. I'll fix something up right away."

The boys sit at the table while Tim heats something up in the kitchen.

"I've been worried sick for you boys, I tell you. But, I'm glad to see that you're all together and safe."

"Uncle, some idiot judge awarded custody to our mother—just because," Stanley said. "But, matters went from bad to worse."

Tim enters the room with plates of food. "Where is your mother?"

"Dead," Hank said.

"Dead? How?"

"We killed her, and her boyfriend, too," Stanley said.

"Oh, well, I guess you had to do it."

"Yes, uncle we had to do it."

"Well, then, you did good."

The boys stuff their mouths for a few moments.

"Uncle, we need you to establish an alibi for us," Stanley said as he chewed a mouthful.

"Sure, anything for you boys. You're blood."

"Well, you like the car we pulled up in?"

"Yeah, I guess."

"Buy it from us."

"Are you sure about this?" Hank asked.

"Very sure. Uncle, buy the car from us and register it in your name. I have the title, and I can sign it over to you right after we're done eating."

"Ah, okay."

"That Malibu rides well?" Stanley asked.

"It rides real well. Why? You want it?"

Yeah, we can consider it a fair exchange with a little cash to help grease the rails."

"Let me get the title."

"No, you remain the owner by title, okay?"

"Stanley, the police are going to question Uncle Tim about Estelle and Travis," Hank said.

"That's the point. Uncle, when the sheriff arrives to question you, you tell him that you have maintained a friendship with Estelle throughout the years. A few weeks ago, she called to offer you a deal on her boyfriend's car. The sale was too good to pass up. So, they came by and made the sale happen. You paid them, say, five hundred dollars in cash. After the sale, they said something about going to Boca del Rio, Mexico. You said your goodbyes, and then they drove off in a red convertible. You haven't seen them since. It's that simple."

"Okay, sounds simple enough." Tim smiles at them. "You boys want seconds?"

An hour later, the boys say goodbye to their Uncle Tim.

"Take care of that car, boys. And, here..." Tim takes out something wrapped in an oily rag. "Take this with you for protection."

Hank opens the rag and sees a pistol.

"And, here's the ammo." He gives the boxes to Jan. "It was a present from your father to me. I think you boys should have it."

They embrace. They load up their new wheels and ride off. They look behind to see Uncle Tim waving at them.

* * *

Just before leaving the county line, they stop at a Koko-Loco donut shop. They notice a deputy sheriff's cruiser parked on the side. So, the boys duck down a little and wait for the officer to leave.

When the officer exists the shop, they notice him. They recognize his face.

"That's him," Stanley said.

"Are you sure?" Jan asked.

"Yeah, that's him," Hank said.

"What are we going to do?" Jan asked.

Neither brother answers Jan. They just watch Deputy Lowe as he gets into his cruiser with a bucket-sized coffee and a bag of fried dough. He starts up the car and drives off. Hank puts the car in gear and follows the cruiser. The boys continue to stay silent, as though the three were operating as one mind.

They then see the officer park at a speed trap, set up his radar, and then recline in his seat. He starts on his second doughnut when Hank parks at his blind spot about fifty feet back.

The boys check their pistols, and then swiftly and carefully approach the cruiser.

Hank approaches at the driver's side and points his pistol at the officer. Lowe looks up and slowly raises his hands.

"Come out! Now!"

The officer steps out.

"What are you doing?"

"Come this way, Deputy Lowe," Stanley said at the other side of the cruiser.

The officer turns and looks over at him, then he looks at Hank.

"Hey, I know you boys. What are you doing?"

Hank takes the officer's pistol and crams it into his waistband while Stanley continues to point his pistol at the officer's head.

"The keys are still in the ignition, so I'll take his car."

Hank nods. "Come with me, officer. Stanley, follow us."

Hank takes Lowe to their car. He binds him with his own handcuffs and puts him into the backseat. Jan also sits in the backseat and holds his pistol to Lowe's head while Hank takes the driver's seat.

Hank drives, as Stanley follows closely, to a remote lake in the woods. Their father used to take them there to swim and fish. They remove Lowe and handcuff him to a tree. Hank then puts the cruiser in neutral, and the boys push it into the lake where it steadily sinks and disappears into the brackish water. They then turn to Lowe.

"I bet you didn't think you'd see us again," Hank said.

"Boys, you'll never get away with this. It doesn't matter that you're young. You'll be caught and, if you're caught alive, you'll spend the rest of your lives in prison—all of you."

"But, you killed our father!" Jan said. "You killed him when he was surrendering."

"It wasn't like that. It was a very dangerous situation that your father put all of us in."

"You can't talk your way out of this," Hank said.

"Killing me won't bring back your father. But, there is a chance for you to escape from his shadow. There's always a chance. All you did was destroy government property—that's nothing. You'll get probation. But, once you cross a dangerous line, there is no way to cross back."

Stanley pulls out a knife. He walks over to Lowe. Just before the officer can offer another word, Stanley jabs the knife into the top of his head. Blood fountains upward and runs down Lowe's face. He groans loudly, jerking and kicking.

The boys watch him as he slips away into unconsciousness. As he dies, they think of their father.

Jan looks over the lake and, in his mind, he sees his father laughing and playing with him in the water. Jan no longer feels helpless; he smiles. He looks back at Lowe. He notices that his body is not entirely lifeless. He raises his pistol, the one that Uncle Tim gave him, and fires into the officer's head. The shot kills him instantly.

"What did you do?" Stanley asked Jan. "Why did you do that?"

"We wanted to prolong this, you fuck!" Hank shouted.

"I don't know. I just think that dad is at peace now, and nothing more was necessary."

"You're a dick," Hank said. "Uncuff him." He gives him the key.

"I'll go find a large rock," Stanley said.

"Find two; I don't want him to ever surface," Hank said as he put away his pistol.

Stanley takes the pistol from Jan and wedges it into his waistband. "Bring me a large rock," he tells him.

After the body sinks, they wait a moment for all the bubbles to stop. They hear the birds fluttering at the far end of the lake. They then look up and notice how dark it has become.

"We need to leave Tipton County immediately," Stanley said.

"All right," Hank said. "Let's go."

The boys walk off with Jan following closely behind. Jan looks back at the lake for a moment.

Chapter 7

Shelby County—much of it, thus far—consists of green meadows, rolling hills, and lavish estates. As the Beltrane boys ride through this countryside, all three consider that they would find greater comfort in amassing more money before leaving the country for new lives. Gaining access to a few homes and obtaining what they need is essential and this thought entirely dominates their minds.

"In there, Jan, there's more of what we need," Stanley told him as he sipped a tea in a large paper cup. He bites the cup so intensely that it nearly rips apart.

"I see," he answered. "But how?"

"We case them to determine a time when no one is home. They don't expect anyone to simply walk into their homes, and that will play to our advantage. Apathy."

After picking up some drive-thru burgers and then driving a few more miles, they park near a huge home that has only one vehicle—a minivan—parked in its desolate, extra-wide driveway.

Halfway through their meal, they notice a woman and small boy leave this house, board the vehicle, and ride away. The boys carefully watch it pull out and disappear down over a small hill toward a main road.

"Okay, now's our chance," Hank said as he shoved the burger wrapper into a paper bag. He drives gingerly up to the house. He puts the car in park and leaves the engine running.

"Jan, stay with the car and wait for us," Stanley said.

"But, I want to help."

"If you stay here and keep on the lookout, you are helping."

Jan nods.

"Let's go," Hank grunts.

Both boys exit the car. Hank goes into the trunk and gets the still blood-stained crowbar. He walks up to the front door and violently levers it open in one move. They enter and get to work.

Stanley, while in the master bedroom upstairs, finds two jewelry boxes full of valuables. After opening some drawers, he finds over two thousand dollars in cash. He then walks back downstairs to the kitchen. He sees Hank squatting in the middle of the floor defecating. Stanley enters just when the feces drop on the floor.

"What the fuck are you doing?" Stanley asked.

"I think it was the burger. I'm almost done."

"It's not necessary, idiot! Let's go!"

"I said I'm almost done!"

When he is done, he wipes with paper towels and tosses them on the floor.

"Hank, let's go now, c'mon!'"

"No, wait! Let's take the blender."

"What? Why?"

"So we can make tropical drinks in our room."

He unplugs the appliance and carries it with him. They get in the car and ride off.

"What did you get?" Jan asked with excitement.

"A few thousand, but your brother took a blender. *Oohh!*"

"Fuck you! When I make some drinks, you're going to want one. You'll see."

* * *

The boys enter Decatur County. They are thinking of the same crime and the same approach. But, they are hoping for a bigger payoff.

They ride past some huge homes until they find one in particular that has all of the telltale signs of being unoccupied: no vehicles, no lights.

They slowly pull into the driveway without saying a word. Hank and Stanley step out and walk around to the side door. Hank crowbars the door open, and they enter.

Inside Stanley hastily takes to the stairs and goes into the master bedroom. After taking a few hundred dollars in cash from a dresser, he finds a sizeable box in a closet. Within it, he uncovers a cache of various valuable items, jewels and precious medals. He finds a shotgun. He decides not to take it, but he does unload it. He then picks up the box and goes downstairs.

He looks around for Hank. "Where are you?"

Hank walks in from one of the back rooms with a small box.

"I found weed," he said. "Look!"

"We have to go!"

"Wait, I need to shit."

"What?"

"It will only take a minute."

Hank dodges into a bathroom and closes the door. For a moment, Stanley is uncertain over what to do. Wait for him by the bathroom door? Go to the car with the stolen goods and wait for him there? He quickly decides to wait for him by the door, but not without keeping an eye out in case the homeowners return.

After a few minutes, Stanley grows impatient.

"We need to move!"

"One second!"

"I'll fucking leave you here!"

"No, you won't."

Stanley then hears some rattling coming from inside the bathroom.

"What are you doing in there?"

"There's some interesting meds in here."

"Come on!"

The bathroom door opens and Hank is cradling medicine bottles. He then reaches around a wall and picks up liquor bottles that he already bagged.

"Some great stuff here," he said.

Stanley just turns and walks out of the house carrying the box. He places the box in the trunk, sits in the backseat and folds his arms. Jan sits in the front passenger seat as Hank gets behind the wheel. He hands his items to Jan.

"What's this?" Jan asked.

"Booze," Hank responded. "I don't know what those pills are, but maybe we can find out later."

As they ride off and out of the long driveway, they notice a car coming from the other direction. After the car passes them, Stanley looks behind to see the car pull into the driveway that they came out from.

"Step on it!" he said.

"What?"

"The owners are just arriving home behind us. So, step on it!"

Hank accelerates to the main road.

"South, we want to go south!" Stanley barked.

"Where?"

"Make a right turn!"

Hank turns right and they speed away.

"I'm hungry," Hank said.

* * *

For the night the boys are staying in a rather drab, but adequate, motel room. The roar of a blender could be heard from the bathroom.

"Jan, hand me another can of coconut milk," Hank shouted over the noise.

Jan goes into the bathroom with a can and joins Hank.

Stanley turns up the volume on the TV as he intently watches the news. He then sees a small cloud of smoke propagate toward him from where his brothers are toiling. He then smells it.

"I think you are celebrating prematurely," Stanley called out to them.

Jan comes back into the room looking quite intoxicated. He looks at Stanley and bursts into laughter.

"Real fucking funny, Jan. Hank, is it necessary to get Jan so high?"

Hank sticks his head out from the bathroom. "Yes, it's necessary—after all the douchebag has been through? Maybe you should lighten up. Have a smoke, have a drink. What the fuck!"

"I'll celebrate when we're in Boca del Rio."

"Don't worry, we'll get there. Get high!" He laughs.

After an hour of partying, Hank gets restless.

"Jan, do you want to go for a ride?"

"Hank, no, we need to remain low," Stanley said. "We are wanted, and we don't know how much the authority knows. We should only leave here when we're on the move."

"We won't be gone for long. I just want to get some pineapple juice."

Hank takes Jan and they both roll out the door. They drive for about twenty minutes until they come to a street where they see a couple of women loitering about calling at passing cars. They also see a man on the side of the road, watching a pacing.

"You wanna have some fun?" Hank asked.

"Um, what do you mean?"

"You know. Let's get ourselves a woman."

"I don't know, Hank. I don't think so."

"Oh, come on."

Hank pulls up alongside one of the women.

"Hey, we want a date," Hank said.

The woman looks at the boys and cringes. "Aren't you fellas a little too young?"

"We're a little young, but we're experienced."

"I don't think so, boys. Maybe you should go on home."

Hank unzips his pants and shows her his penis. It's rather large for a boy of his age, and she reacts to it.

"Mm, looks good, but I don't think so."

Hank then takes out a wad of bills and shows it to her.

"Um, okay," she responded. "I'll go with you."

She gets into the backseat.

"Hey, boys," she said. "How are you tonight?"

"Horny." Hank accelerates so quickly that the tires screech. She flies backward. The man on the side of the road stops pacing and watches attentively as the car rides away.

"Hey, where are you boys taking me?" she said as she sits up.

Hank takes out a pistol from the glove compartment.

"We're going somewhere nice and safe where we're going to have some fun. You'll be paid real well. So, sit back and relax."

The woman nervously sits back.

After a few minutes, Hank finds a vacant lot. It's nearly dark; whatever illumination they receive is from a distant street light.

"Here we are. Now, lady, take your clothes off."

"It doesn't work that way, baby."

"I said take your fucking clothes off!"

As she proceeds to disrobe, Hank gives the pistol to Jan.

"Hold this on her, okay? I'm going to get back there and get some work done."

Jan holds the pistol as Hank enters the backseat. Hank takes his pants down and pushes her head into his penis. She looks up at Jan for a moment before her head moves down. Jan sees the look on her face. She has the look of fear. As she engages in oral sex, Jan thinks of the time Travis was having sex with his mother. The memory disgusts him. He then realizes that what he is now looking at is equally disgusting.

As quickly as it started, the act is over. Hank gets back into the front seat and takes the pistol back.

"All right, now you."

"I don't know."

"Come on, bro."

Jan reluctantly sits in the backseat. He takes down his pants and removes his penis. The woman begins to engage. However, Jan is not getting erect. He wants to stop her, but he also wants to impress his older brother.

"This isn't working," she said.

"What do you mean it's not working?" Hank asked. "You're a pro, right?"

Hank then looks down to see Jan's flaccid penis. "You don't like it?"

"No, I'm not liking this," Jan said with a trembling voice. "I want it to stop."

"No boner bro? What's wrong with you?"

"I guess I'm just nervous."

Hank laughs aloud. "I know, it's because she's so fucking ugly."

"No, it's not that."

"Yes, it's because she's so ugly. She's a fucking disappointment." He points the gun in her face. "Get out."

"What?"

"Get the fuck out the car!"

"What are you going to do?" she asked as she began putting her clothes back on.

"Just hurry up and get the fuck out!"

The woman finished dressing and stepped out of the car. She began to walk away slowly. Hank then steps out of the car and walks over to her. She then removes a razor from her jeans and cut him across the cheek. Blood quires from the gash. She runs away, as fast as she can. But, Hank then takes aim at her and fires. She falls to the ground. He walks over to her limp body and fires one shot into her back and another shot into her head. He kicks her body over and looks at the dead expression on her face. He then walks back to the car while holding his face wound. He gets behind the wheel and rides back to town.

On the side of the road, Hank finds the man. The man looks at them and then looks around for the woman. He glances back at the boys and offers them a "what-the-fuck?" look. Hank draws his pistol and points it at his face.

"Bad quality," Hank said. He then pulls the trigger.

The man instantly falls to the sidewalk. Hank laughs aloud and quickly drives off.

* * *

Sheriff McLean intensifies his search for Deputy Lowe after some of his initial leads go nowhere.

During the preliminary investigation, he interviewed the clerk at the Koko-Loco donut shop. The clerk didn't notice anything out of the ordinary.

In fact, he commented on the officer's sizable appetite.

While parked near the deputy's regular speed trap, McLean picks up a faint tire track of the cruiser, but nothing more. He wonders where the investigation will take him, if anywhere. Thus far, there are no other leads.

* * *

In the motel room, the next morning, Stanley is up early watching the news. When he returns to the TV after going to the bathroom, Hank already changed the channel to watch Tom and Jerry cartoons.

"Hank, I need to watch the news. We need to know as much as we can about what's going on out there."

"I don't care; I want to watch my show."

Stanley manages to take the remote control and change the channel back to the news.

"A woman was found dead in an empty lot this morning. Police say she was shot several times at the scene, and that there may be evidence of sexual abuse. No one has been apprehended... Also this morning, Sheriff Jack McLean of Tipton County continues his search for one of his deputies. Deputy Jonathan Lowe mysteriously disappeared on September 9th without a trace. If anyone has information related to this case, you are asked to immediately contact the Tipton County sheriff's office at..."

"There, you happy?" Hank said. He takes back the remote control and changes the channel back to Tom and Jerry and turns up the volume.

Jan wakes up to the noise.

"Good morning, sunshine!" Hank said to Jan loudly. He then finds a half-smoked marijuana cigarette and lights it up. He draws in some smoke and passes it to Jan.

Jan draws in the smoke, coughs, and then hands the cigarette to Stanley, but he refuses to take it.

* * *

While Sheriff Brooks investigates the disappearance of Estelle Holloway and Travis Elkner, he learns through the Indiana Bureau of Motor Vehicles that Tim Beltrane, the younger brother of Lee, has registered Travis' car as the new owner. Brooks travels to Tipton County to interview him.

"Hello, Mr. Beltrane. I'm Sheriff Earle Brooks from Hancock County. How are you doing today?"

"I'm fine, sheriff. Do you want to come in?"

"Certainly, thank you."

Brooks enters and Tim guides him to the dining room table.

"Have a seat. Would you like some coffee?"

"Yes, please. Black."

"Black it is."

Tim pours the coffee in the kitchen and brings it to Brooks."

"Is this about my brother, Lee?"

"Not exactly. Have you seen his ex-wife, Estelle, lately?"

"Yeah, I seen her a few weeks ago. We remained friends after the divorce. Is she okay?"

"Um, I don't know. I was hoping that you can help me with that."

"What do you mean?"

"Well, she seemed to have disappeared. We're not sure to where, and I was hoping that you can help us."

"When she saw me she did have her boyfriend with her. His name is Travis. She called me some time ago because he had a car to sell, and she wanted me to get in on a really good deal. When they visited, they sold me the car and they drove away together in a red convertible."

"Do you own another car?"

"Ah, yeah, but it's in the shop. It's always breaking down. That's why I needed another car."

"Your other car is a Chevy Malibu."

"Yes, sir. It's a Malibu."

"I see. I have that information here." Brooks looks down at a printout of that car. "Did Estelle and Travis say where they were going?"

"They mentioned something about moving to Boca del Rio, Mexico. They didn't say much else. Then they drove off happy as can be, and I haven't seen them since."

"Okay, Mr. Beltrane," Brooks said as he stood. "I won't take up any more of your time."

"Sure thing, sheriff. If I hear anything, I'll be sure to let you know."

"I appreciate that. Oh, and one more thing: have you seen any of your nephews, Henry, Stanley, or Jan?"

"No, sir. I haven't seen them for some time now."

"All right. Good day, sir."

"Good day, sheriff."

As Brooks walks down the steps, he clutches the printout of the car. He looks at it again and then looks around.

"Chevy Malibu."

Chapter 8

A day later, the boys reach Jennings County. After they check into a motel room, they quickly haul all of their stolen property into the room. Stanley elects to stay behind while Hank and Jan go out for supplies.

As they drive down a side road, they see a young couple on the side of the road that appear to have engine trouble. Hank looks at Jan and then pulls over in front of them. They step out of the car and approach the couple.

"Having problems?" Hank asked.

"Yeah, something wrong and I don't know what it is," the young man answered.

Hank sees the young woman, and he's immediately attracted to her.

"Did you call for a tow?"

"No, not yet. It just happened."

Hank looks at Jan and then draws his pistol. "How 'bout we go into the woods here?"

"What?" the young man asked. "What are you talking about? Is this a joke?"

"No joke. Just do it."

The young couple quickly embrace as they slowly walk into the nearby woods.

"Keep your hands raised."

The couple complies.

When they arrive in a secluded area, Hank gestures to the couple.

"Take their cell phones. Take whatever they have on them."

Jan walks over to them and searches them thoroughly. He uncovers a cell phone and a wallet from the young man.

"The keys are in the car, man. If you can start it, take it and go."

"Hold on a second, do you think you're in charge?" Hank takes out the handcuffs and gives them to Jan. "Handcuff him to the tree."

Jan takes the cuffs and does what Hank orders. Hank then gives the pistol to Jan.

"Just hold it to his head."

Jan walks over to the young man and holds the pistol to his temple.

"Okay, ma'am? Strip," Hank demanded.

"What?" she asked with a trembling voice.

"If I have to ask you again, your boyfriend loses his head."

The young woman cries as she quickly takes off her clothes.

"No! Please!" the young man screamed.

Hank picks up one of the young woman's socks and ties it around the young man's mouth. He then walks up to her and caresses her breasts. He takes them into his mouth, and then squeezes her buttocks. She cries more and more with his every action.

"Shh!" Hank ordered.

She labors to comply with his demands, but with his every touch, she finds it increasingly difficult to contain her disgust.

He forces her on her knees. He then takes out his penis and forces her head toward it.

"C'mon. Do it!" He then turns to Jan. "Get ready to blow his fucking head off if she refuses."

As Jan steadies the pistol, he never takes his eyes off the young man.

It is not long before Hank is done. "All right! Your turn, bro."

Jan shakes his head.

"Oh, come on! She's real good. And, she's a lot prettier than the last one."

The young man struggles with anger.

Jan presses the muzzle tightly against the young man's forehead. He yells at him. "Stop moving! Just stop it! Or, I'll kill you, man!"

"Relax, bro. Come over here and give me the pistol."

Jan walks over to Hank. The girl is sitting on the ground whimpering. Hank takes the pistol from him.

"Now, take out your dick and let her suck it. We don't have all day."

Jan takes it out and presents it to the young woman. She returns to her knees and engages in oral sex. After a few moments, with Jan's eyes tightly shut, the act begins to feel good to him. He is enjoying it. After a minute, he reaches a climax. The semen runs down her face intermingling with her tears and his brother's semen. She sits back down on the ground again. She wipes her face and eyes the best that she can.

"Okay, good work, bro. I'll make a man out of you someday."

To impress his brother further, he takes the young man's cell phone and starts taking photos of the couple. He takes them at various angles, but all capture the horrified expressions on their faces. However, unintentionally, Jan takes a picture of his own face. He is unaware of this as he tosses the cell phone into the woods.

"Time to go," Hank said. He walks over to the young woman and shoots her once in the head killing her instantly. The young man kicks and jerks violently. Through the sock bound to his face, his words escape him in the form of grunts. Hank walks over to him and shoots him once in the head. His body immediately becomes lifeless, and it slouches down and dangles from the tree.

"Take the handcuffs," Hank directed Jan.

Jan takes the cuffs. He puts them in his pocket as he follows his brother back to their car. During all this time, Jan didn't say a word.

* * *

Sheriff Brooks continues his search for the Beltrane boys. He is a little curious about the whereabouts of Tim's Malibu. But, he doesn't think he will investigate that any further. Tipton County is out of his jurisdiction, and he believes Sheriff McLean has enough on his mind with a missing deputy. He does manage to contact the sheriff of Shelby County concerning the boys, but the best he can do is direct his deputies to keep a watch for them, nothing more.

Just as Brooks is about to leave his office for the day, he receives a phone call.

* * *

Frustrated by their lack of success with the amount of money and valuables that they have garnered from residential burglaries, the boys decide to try their hand at armed robbery. They resolved to obtain at least an additional twenty thousand dollars in cash. According to Stanley, that amount may put them in a comfortable financial situation when they arrive in Mexico to start new lives.

In a sporting goods store, they purchase some ski masks. Hank wants to buy one that has a fashionable logo on it, whereas Stanley insists on getting one that is more nondescript so it may be a bit less memorable to the ones they rob. Although Jan will stay in the car while they work, he gets a mask, too. Stanley buys him a plain, black one.

Late at night, they spot a convenience store down a rather dark road but very close to a highway. They see a car parked in the rear and presume that the clerk owns it. Stanley slashes two of its tires with the knife. They then drive around front and see two cars parked in the lot. After five minutes, both cars leave.

"Okay, let's go!" Stanley said. He draws back the top slide of his pistol and puts his mask on.

Jan puts his mask on and takes the driver's seat as the masked Hank exits.

Both boys enter the store and draw their weapons on the clerk. Stanley doesn't speak, but he gestures to the cash register.

The clerk raises his hands and walks over to the register and presses a few buttons to open the drawer. It opens with a thud.

Stanley turns to Hank who is taking some beef jerky and candy bars. Stanley quickly realizes that his brother is not staying on task. So, he walks around the counter to get the cash himself. In doing so, he walks into a blind spot that allows the clerk a narrow opportunity to obtain a pistol from under the counter. He hastily fires. The shot strikes Hank in the upper arm delivering him backwards into some shelves. Groceries fly off and onto the floor. Stanley comes into view with enough time to fire his weapon. He shoots a bullet into the clerk's head. The man immediately drops to the floor.

Stanley then runs to Hank who is steadily bleeding. The bullet appears to have gone through the arm and imbedded itself into the floor.

"Just put pressure on it," Stanley said. "I'll get the money."

Stanley runs around the counter, gets a plastic bag, and dumps the cash into it. He then runs back to assist Hank. By that time, Hank picked up the beef jerky and a pack of playing cards.

"Jesus, Hank! Let's go!" Stanley takes hold of him and rushes him out to the car.

Both boys jump into the backseat.

"Drive!" Stanley said.

Jan puts the car in drive and hits the gas. The car goes over a few bumps, which causes Hank to bounce a bit.

"*Ow*—Fuck! Easy, Jan! I'm shot!"

"Just quiet down; it's just a flesh wound."

"You're shot? Oh, no! We're going to the hospital, right?" Jan asked.

Stanley peaks at the wound and sees that Hank needs stitches. "Yeah, I guess so. We passed one a few miles back. Turn here."

Jan turns the wheel suddenly.

"*Ow!* Jan, will you take it easy?"

"Sorry, Hank!"

After a few exits on the highway, they see a sign for the hospital. They take one exit and follow the signs for the emergency room. They drive into the parking lot and park by the door.

Hank is carried in by his brothers—one on each side of him. They enter a quite empty place and quickly approach the triage desk where a girl sits. She is dressed all in white.

"Hello, can I help you?" she asked. She then sees Hank's bloody shirt. "Oh, my? What happened?"

"He fell off his bike," Stanley answered.

"Really? Oh, my!"

"Excuse me, but where is everyone?"

"There is one doctor and two staff members on hand in the back. I'm here in the front. What form of insurance do you have?"

Hank leans over and looks the girl in the eyes.

"My brother is not telling you the whole truth," he said with a soft voice.

"What do you mean?"

"Babe, I was shot."

"You were *shot?*"

"*Shh*, yeah. And, we don't want it reported, you hear?"

"Well, I don't know."

"Look, I think you're real pretty, and I would like you a whole lot if you can help me and my brothers. We're in a bit of a situation."

Stanley and Jan look at each other.

The girl stands up. "I'll take you in the back with me, but your brothers will have to wait here."

Hank turns to them. "Have a seat, boys, and chill."

The girl assists Hank to a secluded area of the emergency room. She draws a curtain and immediately gets to work. Both entry and exit wounds receive two stitches each. She applies a dressing to both wounds. She then injects him with an antibiotic. As she works, Hank strokes her hair and slips in an occasional kiss.

"There, all done," she said with a smile.

"You know, you are the most beautiful girl I have ever met."

"Oh, stop."

"No, really. He gives her a passionate kiss on her lips while she closes her eyes tightly. "What's your name?"

"Carol."

"Carol. It's a pretty name."

She smiles broadly and looks down.

"Carol, is there a place we can go? Some place more private?"

She nods. "What is your name?"

"Hank."

"Hank, come with me."

She leads him to a remote storage room. They quickly embrace, take off some of their clothes, and engage in sex. It is as quick and as quiet as it can be.

When it's over, Hank gives her more kisses as she helps him put on his blood-stained shirt.

"Oh, this won't do," she said. She takes a hospital shirt from a shelf and puts it on him. "There."

"Thank you, Carol. I have to go."

"I hope I see you again."

"Me, too." He leaves the room and runs to the waiting area.

"All good?" Stanley asked.

"Yeah, better than good."

"Oh, great!" Jan said.

"Say, you boys should try getting shot sometime," Hank said with a smile. "It's really not that bad."

* * *

After some meticulous canvassing in several secluded areas and waterways, Sheriff McLean finds Deputy Lowe's police cruiser partially submerged in the shallow lake. Trolling in the water uncovers the mutilated body of the deputy.

Although it is still early in this gruesome discovery, McLean theorizes that the abduction and murder was committed by two bank robbers on the lam from Ohio who are believed to have been passing through Tipton County at the time of Lowe's disappearance.

Chapter 9

A drive through the state of Kentucky proves uneventful. With the exception of a refueling, the purchase of pop and snack cakes, and a bathroom break, the trek was quick and direct.

In Tennessee, they settle in Cumberland County where they obtain a motel room and stretch out.

After a three-hour nap, Stanley counts money on his bed while Hank redresses his wounds as he watches Tom and Jerry. After Hank finishes, he lights up a marijuana cigarette and blows the smoke in sleeping Jan's face. Jan wakes and coughs. Stanley then takes the remote control and changes the channel to the local news.

"A gruesome discovery was made at a secluded lake in Tipton County, Indiana. After a month-long search, Sheriff Jack McLean discovered the body of Deputy Jonathan Lowe at the bottom of the lake. Sheriff McLean is deeming this a homicide and he has stepped up efforts to find the officer's killer or killers. Deputy Lowe joined the department six years ago.

He was last seen alive on September 9th. He leaves behind a wife and two daughters. Bob...

"Fuck!" Hank said. "They found him."

"Yep, he did," Stanley said.

* * *

As the boys ride around casing some places, Stanley talks about Boca del Rio.

"It's the perfect place to escape. The ocean, the weather, the warm Mexican sun."

"Can't wait," Jan said. "Tropical drinks in hand, basking in the sun, fishing, swimming..."

"Shh, wait!" Just then, Stanley sees a respectable-looking home hidden behind a clearing.

"There. Let's look there."

The house is a bit of a distance away, so they will need to turn around and drive closer. The road they're on is wide enough for Hank to made a U-turn.

As they approach the house, they gradually realize that it is currently unoccupied. They look at each other and smile.

"This may be it," Hank said.

"Indeed," Stanley said. "Hank, let me ask you something. Do you need to take a shit?"

"No, but I may have to *leave* one," he said as he laughs. "I'm good."

"That's good, because we need to get in and get out. If this is the mother lode that I think it is, it will provide us with enough money to charter a boat from Mobile."

They park. Hank and Stanley walk over to the side door as Jan takes the driver's seat. With crowbar in hand, Hank opens the door with ease. As they step inside, they smell the sweet odor of lilacs.

"Hank, look for an office on the first floor." Sometimes, people keep money in a desk. I'll go upstairs to the master bedroom. We're looking for cash and jewelry, that's it."

"Fuck you," Hank said with a smile.

Stanley responds with a smirk and then runs upstairs. While there, he opens drawers and closets. He uncovers little cash, but he does find a jewelry box on a small cabinet. He unrolls a small plastic bag from his jacket pocket and puts all of the jewelry in it. Across the hall, he sees a girl's bedroom. He enters and sees a small jewelry box. He empties its contents into the plastic bag. When he enters another room, he hears Jan blowing the car horn. As he runs down the stairs, he calls out to Hank, but he gets no response. Then, Jan enters the house.

"There's a car coming up the road!" he said.

"Hank, goddammit! Someone's coming! Let's go!"

When the boys turn, they see a middle-aged woman and a teenaged girl walk in, both are carrying groceries.

"Oh, my!" the woman exclaimed. She drops one of the bags.

"Now, lady, there's no need to be frightened," Stanley said. "Just step inside and have a seat—both of you."

"I'm going to call the police," she responded.

"No, you're not," Hank said while standing under an archway pointing his pistol at her. "Do as he said and have a seat."

The woman and girl put their bags on the counter and take seats.

Hank looks at the girl carefully and regards her as very attractive. He blows her a kiss.

"What are your names?" Stanley asked.

"I'm Ruth Strickland, and this is my daughter, Emma," The woman said with a trembling voice. "Please take anything you'd like and leave us."

"Anything?" Hank said as he looks at Emma.

"Please don't hurt us. I have some cash, here." She opens her purse on the counter.

Stanley draws his pistol and points it at her. "Stop!"

She quickly raises her hands. "*Noooo*, please? I was getting you the money. Just take it and leave us! Please?"

"Ladies, just come with me," Hank said while gesturing with his pistol. "Let's have a seat in the dining room. I want you to make yourselves comfortable." He then whispers to Jan. "Get the twine from the trunk."

The woman and the girl sit on the dining room chairs. The mother shakes a bit while the girl appears stunned. When Jan returns with the twine, Hank motions to him to tie them to the chairs. He does so.

"What are you going to do with them?" Stanley asked Hank.

"Well, she looks like a tasty treat."

"I'm serious! What are you going to do?"

"I don't know yet, okay? Just pack up the car and park it around back so no one sees it."

Stanley grunts, gets the keys from Jan, and does what he's told. He returns back into the house to see Hank stoking the girl's hair.

"Okay, now what?" Stanley asked sarcastically.

"I still don't know." He gestures to Jan to come closer to him. He whispers into his ear. "I'm going to have a talk with your idiot brother. Hold your pistol on these two. If they cause any problems, shoot the mother."

* * *

Hank and Stanley are in drastic disagreement about what to do with the Strickland mother and daughter. Hank wants to kill them both, but not without having his way with Emma first.

"Let's let the mother live and take the girl," Stanley insisted. "She won't dare call the authorities while she's with us. The girl will be our insurance policy. When we reach Mexico, we'll release her."

"It's too complicated," Hank responded. "Let's just kill them and be done with it. We're wasting time!"

"If we kill them, that means we'll have more on our tail. The FBI may even get involved, and that means we may never be able to leave the country. Let's take her and go!"

After an hour-long stalemate, they hear someone enter the house.

"Honey?" a man said. "Ruth?"

Hank appears and points his pistol at him. "Don't try anything, pal."

"Who are you? Where's my wife?"

"Your wife is fine," Stanley said as he appears. "Your daughter is here, too. She's fine also."

"What do you want?"

"We came in to burglarize your house, but your

wife and daughter came home. They're in the next room."

"I want to see them," the man insisted.

"If you don't relax, I will shoot you," Hank said.

Stanley attempts to calm the man. "I'll take you to your wife and daughter, but then I have to bind you. What is your name?"

"Arnold."

"And, what do you do for a living?"

"I'm a businessman of imports, mainly home goods from furniture to decorative pottery."

"Oh, that sounds nice."

When Arnold sees his wife and daughter he tries to run to them. "Ruth! Emma!"

Hank prevents Arnold from embracing them by smacking him across the face with the pistol. Arnold falls to the floor. Hank points his pistol at him. "Let's get something straight here. You are not in charge, I am. Sit down in this fucking chair and shut the fuck up." He turns to Jan. "Cuff him to the chair. I'm tired of hearing his shit. If he says another word, shoot him in the head."

While Arnold is cuffed, he looks into Jan's eyes. Jan returns a look that says: "I don't like what I'm doing, but I must do what I'm told."

CHAPTER 10

Later that same night, the boys are having a game of poker.

"Two pairs: aces and eights," Hank said.

"Full house: jacks and nines," Stanley said.

"I got nothing, again."

"You totally suck at this," Hank tells Jan.

"Yeah, I do, but whatever."

"So, what's your name again?" Hank called out to the girl.

"Emma."

"Hi, Emma. And, how old are you?"

"I'm fifteen."

"Fifteen? You look a little older."

Stanley shakes his head and looks down at his watch. "It's time for the news. Let's see what's going on out there."

"Are we going to leave in the morning?" Jan whispered to Stanley.

"I don't know, but hand me the remote." Stanley turns on the TV. He changes the channel and turns up the volume.

"The investigation into the homicide of Deputy Lowe of the Tipton County Sheriff's Department has been intensifying. A manhunt has expended to include three states. Leads indicate that the killer or killers may be headed south and may even attempt to leave the country. Sheriff Jack McLean had this to say:

'Our sources tell us that there may be at least two responsible for the murder of Deputy Lowe, and we believe that they may be in Kentucky or as far south as Tennessee. Various agencies from these states and the FBI have been highly cooperative with our efforts to bring the offenders to justice, and I want to take the opportunity to thank them for all their assistance.'

If anyone has information concerning the whereabouts of those responsible, you are asked to call the Tipton County tip line immediately. Their number is..."

"Change this shit. It's depressing me," Hank said.

"For the first time, I agree with you," Stanley retorted.

Hank takes the remote control and changes the channel. He finds Tom and Jerry, he sits back on the couch and relaxes.

Stanley sits next to him. He whispers into his ear. "I think we should remain here for a few days until things die down a little. If we move in the morning, we may easily be captured. All it takes is one checkpoint and we're done."

Hank listens and thinks. "Yeah, maybe you're right."

Stanley exhales a sigh of relief that Hank didn't argue with him. He gets up and goes to the kitchen.

Hank calls out to Jan for all to hear. "That Boca del Rio trip is going to have to wait."

Stanley overhears what Hank said and, as he pours himself a glass of milk, his eyes open wide with disbelief.

Jan leaves the playing cards and sits on a soft chair that faces the Stricklands. He watches over them while attempting to not make eye contact. For a moment, he does look at Emma. She offers him a sympathetic look. He tries not to smile at her, but a small one does escape his lips. Jan's attention is quickly distracted by Hank.

"Emma, you sure are a pretty little lady. Arnold and Ruth, youse outdid yourselves."

Jan quickly looks away from Emma. He is visibly annoyed with Hank's comment.

* * *

Later that night, Jan stays up on watch for a few hours while his brothers sleep in the beds upstairs. The Stricklands sleep still bound upright to the dining room chairs.

To keep from falling asleep, Stanley instructs Jan to walk around. So, he does. As he steps, a wooden floorboard creaks below his foot. It wakes Emma. She looks at him and smiles. He looks down at her and smiles back. She then gestures that she needs to use the bathroom, so he unties her and ushers her there. While she uses the toilet, he peaks in and watches her—as he's been told to do so. She steps out.

"Are you hungry?" he asked her.

"No, but I am thirsty."

"Okay, come with me."

She follows him to the kitchen.

"Just water, please."

He pours her a glass of water from a decanter and hands the glass to her. She quickly drinks.

"Do you want another?"

"Yes, please."

He pours her another. She sips this time.

"I don't like the way they talk to you," she said.

"What? My brothers? Oh, that's just the way they are."

"It's not right that they push you around. I think they're rude—especially the tall one. He talks down to you."

"I know, but I'm used to it."

She sips. "He mentioned something about Boca del Rio."

"Oh, yeah. It's in Mexico. It's where we're going."

"That's where you're going?"

"Yeah. We're going to start new lives."

"It must be a beautiful place."

"I don't know; I never went there."

"I sure would like to go." She sips.

"Really? Why? This looks like a nice home, and your parents seem all right."

"I hate my parents. I hate them both. I want to get out of this place."

"What? Why?"

"My father abuses me."

"How?"

"He hits me, and he touches me."

"Touches you how?"

"He spanks me."

Jan thinks for a moment. "He gropes you?"

"It's inappropriate," she insists; "and he won't stop."

"I'm sorry."

"My mother won't do anything to stop it. She's hopeless."

"Maybe she's afraid."

"I'm not afraid. One day, this past summer, I thought about stabbing him—I hate him so much. That's sick, right?"

"It's not sick. I don't think you're sick. I totally understand you."

"You're sweet. What is your name?"

"Jan. Do you want more water?"

"No, thank you."

"Okay, well, I guess I have to tie you to the chair again."

"I know."

"I'm sorry."

"It's all right. I enjoyed talking with you, Jan."

"Me, too."

They walk back to the chair. She puts her hands behind her back and places her ankles close to the chair legs. After he ties a few knots, she is sturdily affixed to the furniture.

As Jan is about to go back to pacing, Emma speaks to him in a soft voice.

"Good night, Jan."

"Oh, good night, Emma."

They smile at each other.

Chapter 11

Jan sits in the corner of the dining room eating a sandwich. He plays with the crust of the bread and, at times, he even zones out a little.

"Hey, dick! Are you all right over there?" Hank said to him.

Jan looks up at him, but he doesn't answer. He just continues chewing and thinking.

Hank then goes into the living room to watch television. He picks up the remote control and changes the channel so rapidly that you can't tell what's on at all. It's as though he's changing channels just for the sake of doing something.

Stanley appears from the kitchen and walks over to Jan.

"Finish up. I want you to stay on watch for another hour. Then, I'll take watch so you can get some sleep."

Jan nods.

Stanley goes back into the kitchen.

Even though Jan's sandwich is not even half eaten, he pushes the plate aside and walks over to the Stricklands. He leans over Arnold to check his knots. While doing so, Arnold whispers something in his ear.

"I know you're not like they are. I know you are a just person. Please help us."

Jan shakes his head and then continues to check the knots. All secure. He then sits in the chair facing them. He looks down with a somber look.

"I bet you want a piece of that, huh?" Hank said as he walked by, referring to Emma. "I sure do!" He laughs.

There is no change in Jan's expression.

Hank is oblivious to Jan's mood as he makes sucking noises with his tongue and mouth. As he walks past Jan, he gives him a pat on his chest. "Don't worry—you'll have some of that soon enough."

* * *

Later that night, Stanley is on watch. He looks at Emma as she sleeps. He is a bit captivated by her good looks; he wonders how it must feel to kiss her lips and hold her slender body close to his. He doesn't realize it but, after a few moments, she had awoken and she's looking at him.

"Oh, sorry. I didn't mean to stare."

"It's okay. I have to use the bathroom."

"All right."

He carefully unties her and takes her by the hand gently guiding her toward the bathroom.

"I'm able to walk," she said with a giggle.

"Oh, no problem." He lets go of her hand, and she walks into the bathroom and sits on the toilet. He watches her through the partially-opened door. He tries to get a look at her nakedness but, before he thinks he can, she quickly stands and flushes.

When she emerges, she looks at Stanley and smiles at him. He is uncertain what to say. All he can do is smile back at her.

"Say, everything is going to be fine with you and your family. You all seem like nice people. We only need a little more time and then we'll leave."

"I know. I don't see you as a bad person."

"No, I'm not. We're not. We just need a little time."

"You're very smart. I think you're the smartest one." She offers him a tender smile.

"Yeah, well, I'd like to think so myself. I will make certain that nothing happens to you."

"I believe you."

"Well, come on. I have to tie you to the chair. I'm sorry."

"Do you usually tie up girls?"

Stanley does his best to hold back a laugh. "Now that I think about it—maybe I shouldn't answer that question." He looks back into her eyes.

She walks back to the chair and gets into position. He binds her well.

"Maybe you should get some sleep," he said.

"I'll try."

Stanley sits in the chair facing them. He quickly realizes that Emma is a special girl. He feels the urge to want her, to protect her. Also, he realizes that it would be best to allow her parents to live and take her with them to Mexico. Perhaps she may want to stay him and be his girlfriend. He believes that the way she looks at him conveys that he has a legitimate chance with her.

Chapter 12

Day three in the Strickland home.

Although Stanley and Jan effectively hide their individual feelings for Emma, they collectively look upon Hank as a threat to the girl.

After Stanley engages in some intense thought, he confronts Hank.

"We need to talk in private," he said.

"Not now."

"Yes, now. All three of us. Jan, come over here."

Hank displays an angered face.

"Look, we need to allow the parents to live," Stanley said sternly. "But we must take Emma with us to ensure that they won't notify the authorities. We harm no one."

"I agree," Jan said abruptly. I care about Emma and I don't want anything bad to happen to her."

"What makes you think you will ever have Emma?" Stanley asked Jan.

"Both of you can go fuck yourselves. What is wrong with you? Have you boys gotten soft? When we reach Mexico, we'll have all the pussy we want! We take them out—all of them—and then we quickly make our move south. That's it!"

"No, I won't allow you to kill anyone!" Stanley insisted.

"I give up," Jan declared. "I don't care anymore what you come up with. I no longer want to participate in any discussion because it doesn't matter what I say."

"Smart move," Hank tells Jan. He turns to Stanley. "Maybe you should listen to him."

"It's not necessary to kill them."

"You know, all this talking has made me tired. I'm going to bed." Hank yawns audibly as he climbs up the steps.

Stanley looks at Jan. "You have watch. I'm going upstairs, too. If Hank comes down, you call me."

Jan gives him a halfhearted hand salute.

* * *

Late in the night, while Jan is on watch, he wakes Emma.

"Come with me!" he whispered to her as he unties her.

"What are you doing?"

"We have to leave now. Let's go!"

She carefully and quietly walks with him as he gets the car keys. Also, he leaves the handcuff key on the counter. Emma sees him do this.

They make their way outside and walk around back some distance away from the house to the car. As she sits in the passenger seat, he looks in the trunk. He confirms that all the cash and valuables are there. He gets in the driver's seat and starts it up. They ride around to the driveway in the front of the house.

Hank and Stanley don't hear them leave until they reach the driveway. By that time, Jan and Emma ride off in the direction of the main road. The brothers awaken and quickly run down the stairs. At the bottom of the stairs in the dining room, all they see is Arnold and Ruth. They are sitting up and appear to be still bound to the chairs.

"What the fuck is going on?" Hank yelled at them. "Where is your daughter?"

Stanley runs outside and quickly comes back into the house.

"The car's gone! They took everything!"

"What? That little fuck!" Hank turns to Arnold. "Give me the keys to your car."

"I don't have them. He took the keys to both of our vehicles."

"What did Emma tell you?" Stanley asked them.

"She didn't tell us anything!" Ruth said.

"What do we do?" Hank asked Stanley.

"I don't know."

"I should of killed them when I had the chance, Stanley!"

"What do you mean, Hank? You caused this! You scared Jan off and now we're stuck here. You're going under, you fuck!"

Hank immediately punches Stanley in the face so hard that his brother falls to the floor at Arnold's feet. He is motionless.

To Hank's surprise, he sees Arnold out of the handcuffs reaching for Stanley's waistband. Arnold pulls out Stanley's pistol—the same pistol that Uncle Tim gave them—and points it at Hank's head.

"You fuck!" Hank said while clenching his teeth. "You think you're going to shoot me? You don't have the fucking guts!" He then goes into his waistband for his pistol.

Arnold immediately pulls the trigger shooting Hank in the head. Blood sprays from the wound as he falls to the floor.

Ruth screams.

When Stanley rises from Hank's punch, Arnold quickly shoots him in the head, too. Blood missiles from the bullet hole as he falls dead next to his brother.

Chapter 13

Mobile harbor is a bustling marine-travel capitol that can be sizably compared with nearby New Orleans harbor.

Jan and Emma complete a transaction to charter a boat that will take them to Veracruz harbor. Paid entirely in cash, with no questions asked.

While they stand on the deck of the boat, they look out at the vast, blue gulf. They embrace. They take in the salty air. They are free to create their own future together.

* * *

After a few days, they are seen strolling on the beach in Boca del Rio. They are now lovers.

They have not been honest about their age to the resident folks. They drink the local drinks, and they celebrate their independence. They stay at a nearby motel while they talk about purchasing a villa.

As they walk hand in hand, a man approaches them. He is dressed in a seersucker sport coat and he wears a beige, wide-brimmed hat that is pushed down slightly over his sunglasses. He speaks to them.

"Hello."

"Hello," Emma responded.

"Young man, do you remember me?"

Jan looks at him carefully. "No. Should I know you?"

"Well, I'm Earle Brooks."

Jan thinks. "Oh, yeah, I know you. But, what are you doing here? You're not here to take me back, are you?"

Brooks ignores the question. "Do you remember that young man you killed on the side of the road?"

Jan remembers.

"That was my son."

Jan's mouth hangs open. "I—I didn't know."

"And, do you remember the young woman that he was with? The one that you raped and killed?"

He nods, frightened.

"She was carrying my grandchild."

Jan takes a breath and swallows. "So, you're here to arrest me."

"You see, you committed a capital offense that may subject you to the death penalty. So, Mexico would not allow extradition. So, no. I'm not going to arrest you."

Brooks draws a pistol from his coat and shoots Jan in the head. His lifeless body quickly drops to the sand.

Rancorous